WINTER AT STONEFIRE

Dragon Clan Gatherings
Book 2

JESSIE DONOVAN

Winter at Stonefire

Copyright © 2023 Laura Hoak-Kagey

Mythical Lake Press, LLC

Print Edition

www.JessieDonovan.com

Cover Art by Laura Hoak-Kagey of Mythical Lake Design

ISBN: 978-1944776848

The Stonefire and Lochguard series intertwine with one another. (As well as with one Tahoe Dragon Mates book.) Since so many readers ask for the overall reading order, I've included it with this book. (This list is as of August 2023.)

Sacrificed to the Dragon (Stonefire Dragons #1)
Seducing the Dragon (Stonefire Dragons #2)
Revealing the Dragons (Stonefire Dragons #3)
Healed by the Dragon (Stonefire Dragons #4)
Reawakening the Dragon (Stonefire Dragons #5)
The Dragon's Dilemma (Lochguard Highland Dragons #1)
Loved by the Dragon (Stonefire Dragons #6)
The Dragon Guardian (Lochguard Highland Dragons #2)
Surrendering to the Dragon (Stonefire Dragons #7)
The Dragon's Heart (Lochguard Highland Dragons #3)
Cured by the Dragon (Stonefire Dragons #8)
The Dragon Warrior (Lochguard Highland Dragons #4)
Aiding the Dragon (Stonefire Dragons #9)
Finding the Dragon (Stonefire Dragons #10)
Craved by the Dragon (Stonefire Dragons #11)
The Dragon Family (Lochguard Highland Dragons #5)
Winning Skyhunter (Stonefire Dragons Universe #1)
The Dragon's Discovery (Lochguard Highland Dragons #6)
Transforming Snowridge (Stonefire Dragons Universe #2)
The Dragon's Pursuit (Lochguard Highland Dragons #7)
Persuading the Dragon (Stonefire Dragons #12)

Treasured by the Dragon (Stonefire Dragons #13)
The Dragon Collective (Lochguard Highland Dragons #8)
The Dragon's Bidder (Tahoe Dragon Mates #3)
The Dragon's Chance (Lochguard Highland Dragons #9)
Summer at Lochguard (Dragon Clan Gatherings #1)
Trusting the Dragon (Stonefire Dragons #14)
The Dragon's Memory (Lochguard Highland Dragons #10)
Finding Dragon's Court (Stonefire Dragon's Universe #3)
Taught by the Dragon (Stonefire Dragons #15)
Winter at Stonefire (Dragon Clan Gatherings #2)
Masked Dragon of Snowridge (Stonefire Dragons Universe #4 / January 2024)
Charming the Dragon / Hayley & Nathan (Stonefire Dragons #16 / 2024)

Short stories that lead up to *Persuading the Dragon* / *Treasured by the Dragon*:

Meeting the Humans (Stonefire Dragons Shorts #1)
The Dragon Camp (Stonefire Dragons Shorts #2)
The Dragon Play (Stonefire Dragons Shorts #3)
Dragon's First Christmas (Stonefire Dragons Shorts #4)

Semi-related dragon stories set in the USA, beginning sometime around *The Dragon's Discovery* / *Transforming Snowridge*:

The Dragon's Choice (Tahoe Dragon Mates #1)
The Dragon's Need (Tahoe Dragon Mates #2)
The Dragon's Bidder (Tahoe Dragon Mates #3)

The Dragon's Charge (Tahoe Dragon Mates #4)
The Dragon's Weakness (Tahoe Dragon Mates #5)
The Dragon's Find (Tahoe Dragon Mates #6)
The Dragon's Surprise (Tahoe Dragon Mates #7 / TBD)

Chapter One

Jane Hartley pushed her new reading glasses up the bridge of her nose and scanned the contents of her presentation and proposal yet again. She had one chance and one chance only to win over all the dragon clan leaders and get them to agree to her plan. It had to be perfect.

She was so focused on her laptop that she jumped when hands began massaging her shoulders. Her mate, Kai Sutherland, leaned down and kissed her cheek. "You need a break, Janey."

Sighing, she leaned her head back against Kai's firm stomach and looked up at him. "It's nearly done, I promise. I just don't want to fuck this up."

Her mate continued to massage her shoulders as he said, "You won't. I'm helping you, so it can't go wrong."

She rolled her eyes. "And the cockiness comes out again."

His lips twitched. "It's not cocky if it's true."

"Kai, I know what you're doing. But be serious for a moment and think of all the children we'll be helping."

"If you're telling me to be more serious, then I know you've worked too long." She opened her mouth to reply, but he beat her to it. "There's no way the clan leaders will turn away the orphaned dragon-shifters. Not after what we learned about the facility we rescued Percy from."

Just thinking of the half-human and half-dragon-shifter woman who'd arrived earlier in the year only made Jane more determined. Percy Smith—now Wells —had been an orphan sold at age thirteen to a facility where they had conducted experiments and routinely abused her. She hadn't been the only one to suffer, either; some of the former prisoners were still recovering on Stonefire.

Percy had been slow to open up, but eventually had shared more and more with Jane and a few other women on Stonefire about her time inside that place. The truths had only stoked a new fire inside of Jane—to stop orphanages full stop and to have the dragon children living with the dragon clans in the UK and Republic of Ireland. Especially since so many people wanted more children, but some dragon-shifters had trouble conceiving.

Some humans, too, like her.

Before her mind could go down that path again, Kai gently caressed her cheek, and she snapped out of her head as he said, "Come, love. Take a break with me."

She could fight it, but Jane knew her mate was right, that she was more than prepared. After all, she'd spent weeks on this presentation and plan. Her meeting with the clan leaders was the following afternoon, and there was little she could do to improve what she already had.

Jane leaned away from her mate, took off her glasses, and stood. As soon as she was upright, Kai swung her around and pulled her flush against him. He kissed the bridge of her nose. "I rather like your new glasses. Maybe you should wear them to bed."

She raised an eyebrow. "We tried that already, and you broke the first pair."

He smiled at her—one that bordered on a grin, which he only gave to her—and replied, "That was my dragon, not me."

Looping her arms around his neck, she pressed herself more against Kai's hard chest. "Don't make him the scapegoat. You're one and the same. Well, most of the time. He's still the only one who sides with me on the importance of dragon cuddles."

Kai grunted. "And that won't change."

She stood on her tiptoes and whispered, "You say that, but I know exactly how to change your mind." She ran one hand down his chest and over his belly until she could stroke his already hard cock through his jeans. When he sucked in a breath, she squeezed harder. "Because after sex, you always want dragon cuddles."

With a growl, Kai stepped back and swooped Jane into his arms. "I'll take that as a deal, one we need to seal right now."

She laughed. "Of course you want to." She kissed

him gently before adding, "So what are you waiting for?"

Kai didn't waste time dashing up the stairs to their bedroom, laying her on the bed, and shredding her clothes with his talons. She'd learned long ago that scolding him about destroying her jeans and tops did nothing. No, she'd torture him her own way later—with her mouth.

But as her mate kissed every inch of her body, made her come with his mouth, and then claimed her with his cock, she forgot about everything else. Right here, right now, she had the love of her life naked and inside her.

However, despite the fact she came before him— Kai was determined on that point—when he finally growled and stilled inside her pussy, Jane resisted the little pang of sadness that always came recently. They'd tried for nearly a year to have a baby, and not even Sid's fertility treatments had worked.

It came down to the fact that Jane wasn't compatible with dragon-shifters. Sid said that was changing, as her dragon doctor group had all sorts of ideas about how to circumvent that, to make it possible for her and Kai to have a child.

And yet, nothing had worked so far. Kai said he didn't care and that she was all he wanted, but Jane often wondered about that. Especially since a true mate would've been able to give him a child, and she wasn't his.

As Kai hugged her to his side afterward, she pushed aside those thoughts and merely reveled in her mate's presence. Jane fell asleep to images of orphaned children arriving on Stonefire, one or two that might even come live with her and Kai. Because even if she could never give him a child, they could give other children a loving home.

Which was why she had to convince all the clan leaders of her plan.

Chapter Two

The next morning, Dr. Cassidy "Sid" Jackson kissed her son's cheek and handed him over to her mate's brother-in-law, Harris Chisolm. Little Wyatt instantly started squirming, wanting down. Sid smiled. "Are you sure you can handle watching him? If you take your eyes off him for two seconds, he'll find a way out the door and run naked down the footpath."

It'd become one of Wyatt's favorite things to do. Ever since he'd learned to almost run, the little boy took every opportunity to do it. To say he often tired out Sid and her mate, Gregor, was an understatement.

The naked child aspect was new, though, and a bit embarrassing, even if dragon-shifters viewed nudity differently than humans. Being naked to shift was one thing, but streaking across the clan for no reason was another.

Harris smiled at Wyatt. "Aye, it'll be fine. Fiona will tire him out whilst I watch from the sidelines."

Fiona was Harris's daughter. The pair had recently

moved to Stonefire as part of an agreement between her clan and Lochguard for a fresh start.

Since Harris's mate and other daughter had died years ago, Sid couldn't blame him. Although this was still the first time Harris would be watching Wyatt alone, and she was nervous.

Her dragon spoke up. *Don't be. He raised Fiona by himself, ever since his mate died.*

I know. But Wyatt is more than a handful.

Her beast snorted. *He has our determination and stubbornness and Gregor's charm. Of course he's a handful.*

Harris spoke up before Sid could reply to her dragon. "Go, Sid. You and Gregor are going to be busy for the next few days, and I promise Fiona and I can handle Wyatt. Especially since Percy has organized all sorts of events for the children, to keep them occupied. I'll merely be another body in the room, or a pair of arms to catch a wee rascal."

It was true—there were a lot of young children on Stonefire these days, and Bram had ensured the adults could get some much-needed work done this week, during the dragon clan gathering. Along the Percy, Kaylee MacDonald had come down from Lochguard to help watch over the children. Usually Sarah Carter-Wells helped with the young, but she had recently had a baby girl and needed to heal. Plus, Percy was pregnant herself and Bronx had made it clear that unless she had ample help, he'd shadow his mate the entire time and scowl at anyone who asked too much of her. In other words, he'd get in the way and frustrate the hell out of Percy.

On one level, Sid understood Bronx. Just like her

mate Gregor, Bronx had lost his first mate to the perils of pregnancy and childbirth. However, Percy was just learning to open up to the clan and grow into herself, and Sid wouldn't have Bronx sulking about and hindering the female's progress.

She nodded at Harris. "I know." She leaned down and kissed Wyatt's cheek. "Be a good lad for us."

Gregor's Scottish voice drifted into the room. "I'd be okay if he gave Harris a little hell."

Sighing, she turned toward her mate, who instantly pulled her to his side and kissed her. He murmured, "Good morning, love."

Sid raised her brows. "Were you just encouraging my son to be a 'wee hellion', as you'd put it?"

Humor danced in Gregor's eyes. "Your son, is it? Usually, when he's in trouble, he's my son."

She smiled up at Gregor. "Aye."

At her poor attempt to sound Scottish, Gregor laughed. He patted her arse and looked over her shoulder at Harris. "Wyatt's a good lad. And I trust you, Harris."

Sid turned to her side and leaned her head against Gregor's shoulder so she could see Harris and Wyatt again. "I do too. But if anything happens, anything at all, let me know. I don't care if I'm talking to all the clan doctors and in the middle of a heated debate, interrupt me."

Wyatt leaned backward, in an attempt to be let down. Harris tickled his side, and the boy giggled. Harris said, "Aye, I know. We'll be fine. Now, I'm off. Fiona should be awake by now and I know she's eager to see Daisy at the children's events today."

Daisy Chadwick was a human girl who'd moved to Stonefire when her mother had mated a Stonefire dragon-shifter named Blake Whitby. According to Harris, Daisy and Fiona had become fast friends, despite the fact Fiona was much shyer than Daisy.

Sid nodded. "Thanks again, Harris."

Harris waved goodbye, as did Wyatt. Once the front door closed behind them, Gregor nuzzled the side of her head and said, "He'll be fine, Cassidy. Both of them, aye? Ever since moving to Stonefire, Harris has become like he once was—more charming and at ease."

Something Harris hadn't been in a long time, since his mate's death.

Sid bobbed her head. "I know. But asking him to run after a naked little boy, one who'll give him a merry chase and giggle the entire time, is a bit much."

Gregor chuckled. "It's just a phase, and it'll pass." He maneuvered until she was facing him, and he took her cheeks in his hands. "And because Harris collected Wyatt early, we have a little over an hour to ourselves." He leaned down to nip her ear. "And you could do with some relaxing, love. Because I know once all the doctors arrive, I'll have to carry you off to get any sleep."

"Gregor, no carrying me off!"

He chuckled and nipped her jaw. Sid barely suppressed a moan.

Her dragon spoke up. *I want him to carry us. Maybe throw us over his shoulder and then find a nice spot in the woods to bend us over a log and fuck us from behind.*

Before she could think of what to say to her beast,

Gregor murmured, "Your protests won't work on me, Cassidy. I can tell you like my idea." He kissed her neck, and she threaded her fingers through his hair. His hot breath danced across her skin as he said, "So maybe it's time to try it out, aye?"

He nipped her earlobe and then stepped back. In the next second, he had her tossed over his shoulder. Sid was about to protest when he lightly smacked her arse and then rubbed the slight sting.

Gregor nipped her arse cheek and said, "Aye, you want this."

No doubt he could smell her arousal. Sometimes, dragon-shifter senses were a pain in the arse.

Her dragon just laughed.

Her mate adjusted his hold on her and went up the stairs. Sid lightly dug her nails into Gregor's back, both woman and beast wanting to mark him a little to stake their claim.

Her dragon growled. *He's ours already.*

I know. But remember how loud he shouted the last time he came as we scratched hard enough to draw blood?

Yes, yes. Let me out to play, and I'll do a better job.

Sid smiled against Gregor's back. *We'll see.*

Her mate lightly placed her on the bed, on her back, and then kissed her. He took his time tasting her lips, then exploring her mouth and stroking his tongue against hers.

All thoughts of the day or her son fled as Gregor indeed "relaxed" her.

Three times.

Chapter Three

Dr. Layla McFarland had just lifted her son Caelan out of the car seat and onto her hip when a familiar voice shouted, "Layla!"

Smiling, she turned and saw her former mentor, Dr. Gregor Innes, heading toward her, with his mate at his side.

Before Layla had become Lochguard's head doctor, Gregor had occupied the position. For years, she'd watched the male go through the motions and try to hide his pain. However, ever since he'd mated Sid, he'd become a new male. "Hello Gregor, Sid. It's nice to see you in person and not on a screen, aye?"

Layla's mate, Chase, walked to her side with their other son in his arms. He nodded at the doctors in greeting. "Where's wee Wyatt?"

Gregor answered, "With Harris. The offer for Percy, Kaylee, and the others to help watch over your twins is still there."

Chase shook his head. "Thanks, but no. One of our

wee rascals is fussy in new places. And I promised Layla I'd watch over them whilst she worked. It's only fair considering she did the same for me when I had to leave for a job in Inverness for a week."

The week without Chase's help had really shown Layla how much she relied on him. Not just to help with the twins, but also to keep her warm and help her sleep; without Chase, the bed was too cold.

Layla readjusted her grip on her son and said, "Just for the first day. Once Caelan is settled, we might take you up on the offer. The lads could do with making friends on Stonefire."

Chase chuckled. "That won't take long for our wee Harry."

It was true, their son Harry—his full name was Harris, but they always called him Harry—had very much inherited his dad's easy way with strangers. Their other son, Caelan, was a bit more reserved, like Layla had been as a child. Aye, she dealt with all kinds of people as a doctor now. However, it'd taken a lot of work over the years to overcome her initial shyness.

Their two lads were close, though, and the more outgoing one always included the shyer one. It was sweet, really.

Sid nodded. "Then let's get you settled quickly. The other doctors should arrive soon."

Excitement buzzed through Layla's veins. "I can't believe it's finally happening, aye?"

Sid motioned for them to walk, and they all started moving. "It's about time all the head doctors met together. Whilst I understand the clan leaders getting together is important, our group might be even more so."

Layla bit her lip to keep from protesting. Sid was extremely passionate about her ongoing project, where all the dragon-shifter doctors were more open and transparent with one another. Aye, it had made a huge difference. And yet, the clan leaders were the ones to grant permissions and obtain the same from the Department of Dragon Affairs; their cooperation was a wee bit more important, in Layla's opinion.

Chase had rearranged Harry to one side and placed a hand on her lower back. His light touch relaxed her. He said, "I think as time goes on, we'll have meetings of all different groups and occupations. I imagine the teachers would like to meet together too, aye?"

Gregor nodded. "Aye, I think so. Tristan has asked about it, but with all the doctors coming this time, the DDA wouldn't allow more dragon-shifters to gather in one place for a week."

Chase replied, "To even have this many in one spot is progress. Although at the rate Stonefire keeps poaching our clan members, there might not be many of us left to visit."

Layla knew her mate was teasing, and she lightly bumped against his side. "It's not that many. Besides, Lochguard should be welcoming a few from Northcastle soon. And maybe even Glenlough, one day."

Ever since Adrian Conroy had become clan leader of Northcastle in Northern Ireland, he'd been making a lot of changes. His clan also served as a kind of liaison between the Irish dragon clans and the British ones. Well, mostly. True, Aaron Caruso—who was originally from Stonefire—had mated the clan leader of Glenlough. But the other three Irish dragon clans were a wee bit wary of the UK ones.

Her dragon spoke up. *It'll take time. But our primary concern should be the doctors. The sooner we settle everything for the day, the sooner we can snuggle with Chase.*

If the lads fall asleep, Caelan will fuss, to no end.

Her beast grunted. *I still say take up Stonefire's offer and have someone watch them. We deserve a wee break with our mate.*

Layla wanted to. And yet, her two lads were wee miracles she treasured every chance she could. Because of her health, Layla couldn't have any more bairns. Which meant this was the only time she'd experience her children growing up.

Her dragon said softly, *One night will be fine. Of course I love our lads. But we need to take care of ourselves too.*

Now you're sounding like Chase.

Her beast sniffed. *If I push you to look after yourself first, then his dragon won't get the chance.*

Layla nearly smiled. *It's not always a competition.*

Of course it is.

Chase leaned over and whispered, "What's your dragon saying now?"

Caelan said, "Dragon. Dragon. Dragon?"

She smiled at her mate. "Whispering means nothing if your son is right here."

Sid walked over and opened her arms. "Let me carry him a bit. You two drove all the way from Lochguard and deserve at least a few minutes of rest."

Not waiting for an answer, Sid looked over her shoulder. "Gregor?"

Before Layla knew it, the pair had a lad in each of their arms. Maybe she could've protested, but Sid was hard to argue with.

Besides, as she sank against Chase's side and breathed in his comforting scent, she realized how much she needed a few minutes alone with him. Especially since she'd soon have to face all the doctors, most of whom were stubborn. Sid and Gregor might be the hosts, but they all had to speak up and contribute. Otherwise, the meeting wouldn't be that useful.

As soon as Sid, Gregor, and her sons were a few feet away, Chase hugged her against her side. "You'll be brilliant this week, love."

"I know. It's just going to be busy. And it's only the second time I've left Alex in charge of the clan whilst I was away."

Chase kissed her forehead. "He did fine when you came down to help with Percy, aye?"

"I know, but—"

"Ssh, lass. Stop worrying. Besides, I know how much you enjoy talking to the other doctors. This should be like a doctor party, aye? Maybe you need some little skeleton necklaces to wear, a hat with surgery tools tucked in the ribbon around it, or how about a cake shaped like a cock?"

Layla laughed. "Why a penis and not a vagina?"

He waggled his eyebrows. "Do both, and then you can do a wee cake demonstration on how bairns are made."

Trying not to laugh, she lightly hit his side. "Don't be ridiculous, aye?"

"I still say it'd be a way to liven up the meetings."

She laughed again and then stopped, turned, and put her arms around Chase's neck. "Despite your ridiculousness sometimes, I love you."

His pupils flashed to slits and back. "I love you too, lass. And maybe later, we can do a little demonstration of our own, and I can show you just how much."

"Maybe. I might need a kiss first, for some encouragement."

He nipped her bottom lip. "More like a reminder of what'll be waiting for you when you're done."

Her mate kissed her, long and hard, leaving her breathless and her lips swollen. However, Layla didn't mind the reminder. If anything, it made her more open to the idea of taking up Bram's offer to have someone watch their bairns. A few hours alone with Chase wouldn't hurt.

Her dragon grunted. *Finally. I'm going to sleep all day to conserve my strength.*

You were going to sleep all day, anyway. You hate when doctors talk shop.

It's boring. But you love it, so I'll leave you to it.

As her dragon curled up inside her head and fell asleep, Layla merely walked next to her mate and smiled. At one time, she'd thought she would never have time for a mate. And now? She couldn't imagine her life without Chase.

And later, she would show him just how much he meant to her, too.

Chapter Four

Kai Sutherland tried to focus on what his second-in-command, Nikki Gray-Hartley, was saying, but his mind kept wandering back to the night before, when he'd glimpsed sadness on Jane's face. She didn't think he'd noticed, and Kai hadn't asked about it since he didn't want to distract her from her important presentation coming up. However, he never liked seeing his mate unhappy.

His dragon spoke up. *She's stressed.*

It's more than that, dragon.

In truth, Kai wondered if the failed fertility treatments were the cause. Because no matter how often he told Jane that she was all he wanted, she didn't believe him.

His beast huffed. *It's because of our mum.*

Maybe. But after I talked to Mum privately, she stopped asking about grandchildren.

Well, we'll have to find out soon what made her sad. Jane rarely keeps secrets from us.

Not about important stuff. She'll always sneak out to investigate something, if she thinks it's important.

It was true—while Jane had gotten better about letting him know if she had to rush off for a story or information, every once in a while she did it in secret and told him after the fact. Something about it being easier to ask for forgiveness than permission.

As if Kai would ever truly hinder his mate and keep her caged in.

His beast grunted. *In some extreme cases, you would.*

Nikki snapped her fingers in front of his face. "Are you listening, Kai?"

"Sorry, Nikki. Jane has her big presentation later today, and it's on my mind."

Only a half-lie. He hoped more than anything the clan leaders would approve of Jane's idea.

Nikki replied, "I know. But it's bound to go brilliantly. Most dragon-shifters love children, and their old prejudices against half-human dragon-shifters are mostly dead. To be honest, I'm not sure why the DDA didn't suggest we take in abandoned orphans years ago."

He raised an eyebrow. "Really?"

She rolled her eyes. "Okay, okay, yes, things weren't exactly warm between us for a long time. But the relationship between our clan and the DDA has improved and been decent for quite a few years now. If they were still stuck in the past, I wouldn't have Rafe as my mate."

Nikki was mated to a human male named Rafe Hartley, who was Jane's brother. Mating between human males and female dragon-shifters had been rare for decades, until Nikki's case. There were two other such pairings on Lochguard now, although the other clans hadn't embraced the changes quite as quickly. Not all of them were set in their old ways. But Clan Skyhunter in the South of England had gone through a lot in recent years and was clawing their way back from a brutal, dictator-like clan leader. One that had even tortured his own people.

His dragon growled. *I wish we could've had some time alone with that bastard.*

I know. But if we had, then we wouldn't be here for Janey. We'd be in prison.

His beast grunted. *There's a lot you can do without technically breaking the rules.*

Kai nearly smiled, but had to focus on Nikki's words instead as she said, "Let's greet the arriving clan leaders and doctors. Then you can take the rest of the day to be with Jane." He frowned and opened his mouth to protest, but Nikki beat him to it. "I won't take no for an answer, either. You told me that if you were ever distracted about something and needed to spend time with your family, then I could tell you to sod off. Well, this is one of those times, Kai." She smiled. "Take care of your mate." She added in a mock-whisper, "And me being temporarily in charge means I can give Rafe something to do, so he'll stop texting me over and over again to see if I'm okay."

She placed a hand on her extremely swollen belly; Nikki was pregnant with her second child. Something which made his brother-in-law even more bloody irritating since Rafe could be more protective than a dragon-shifter at times.

Kai grunted. "Fine. But if you go into labor this week, I'll never hear the end of it from Rafe. So don't do it."

Nikki chuckled. "As if I can control that. But I'll give my child a talking to. If he or she is like their father, it will take multiple times to make it stick."

Like most dragon-shifters, Nikki and Rafe were waiting to discover the gender of their baby when he or she was born. With two dragon-shifter parents, the odds would favor a boy. However, human male and female dragon-shifter parents tended to have more females. So, only time would tell.

Although Kai hoped it was another girl. Then Rafe would be outnumbered even more. And given the child's parents, she would be stubborn and a handful.

His dragon snorted. *I hope so. It'll be fun to watch.*

Someone knocked, and the door opened, revealing two Stonefire Protectors—Zain Kinsella and Quinn Summers. Zain motioned toward the hallway. "The leaders and doctors flying in are nearly here and will land within minutes."

Kai stood, and Nikki followed suit. He nodded. "Right, then let's get everyone settled."

As they walked out of the Protector building and toward the main landing area, Kai tried his best to forget about Jane's flash of sadness. He needed to get the visitors to their accommodations—each person or couple would stay with a family on Stonefire, as a sort of bonding experience—and then he could go to Jane.

Because as soon as her presentation was finished, he would talk to her. No matter what was going on, he would find a way to make his Janey smile again. He loved her, had told fate to fuck off to have her, and part of his job was making her happy.

Chapter Five

J ane paced inside the small room just off Stonefire's
great hall. All the clan leaders had arrived—plus
the doctors—and had been given time to settle in.
Which meant that in less than ten minutes, Jane would
enter the adjacent room, face all five UK dragon clan
leaders plus the one from Glenlough in Ireland, and
pitch her idea.

She knew the details inside and out, plus what most
of them would ask. And yet, there was no guarantee.
Her clan leader, Bram, loved the idea. But unless all the
leaders agreed to take in the orphans, her plan might
not work. Because no matter how much Bram and
Stonefire wanted to take care of the children, there
wasn't enough room in the clan to shelter all the
orphaned half-dragon-shifter children from the UK
and Ireland, which numbered more than a hundred.

One hundred children abandoned over the years, in
ages ranging from months-old to sixteen. Just the
thought of a child spending sixteen years without a

family made her heart squeeze. Her older brother Rafe might annoy the shit out of her sometimes—okay, most of the time—but they loved each other and would do anything for one another. Every child deserved to be loved.

Thinking of that only made her anxiety worse; failure wasn't an option. Jane's stomach churned, and she rushed to the attached toilet. She barely made it to the bowl before she was sick.

Just as she flushed the toilet, Kai rushed in and kneeled beside her. "Are you okay, love?"

She took a second to breathe in and out, ensuring her stomach was calm. "I'll be fine."

Kai brushed the hair from her face and then stiffened. She glanced at him, and his pupils flashed rapidly. She asked, "What's wrong?"

He cleared his throat. "Nothing. We'll talk after your meeting."

He stood and helped Jane to her feet. After she rinsed out her mouth and washed her hands, she leaned against the counter and sighed. "I've never vomited before a meeting in the past." She shook her head. "No matter. I'm still going to kick ass and take names."

Kai smiled at her. "Of course you are, Janey. If you can convince me to let you investigate slightly dangerous things, you can persuade anyone to do just about anything."

She smiled back at her mate. "Almost. You still won't let me go to Ireland to see how the new dragon clan leaders are doing."

Kai raised his brows. "You might be human and

can travel more easily between countries, but you're mated to me and on the DDA's watchlist. If you enter Ireland and approach the dragon clans without permission, you'll end up in a lot of fucking trouble, Janey."

"Maybe. But just think of it, Kai—to be the first to see how the new Irish leaders are doing without artifice or lies. It would be brilliant, and help out Bram, Finn, and so many others."

"No, Janey. My answer is still no."

She sighed. "It was worth a shot."

He pulled her close and kissed the top of her head. Jane was tall for a woman, and she loved how Kai was even taller and made her almost feel small. She wrapped her arms around his chest and merely took comfort from his familiar heat and scent. Both seemed to calm her stomach.

Kai's voice rumbled under her ears against his chest. "Better?"

"Yes." She lifted her head and met Kai's eyes. A mixture of warmth and happiness filled his gaze, which made her heart warm. "Despite your occasional sternness, I love you."

He gently kissed her lips. "Let's not get into the 'Despite your…' list or it may take a while."

Jane lightly hit his arm. "Be nice."

He laughed, something she could make him do more than anyone else. And it always made her happy to see her growly, serious mate let go a little. She added, "I need to clean up a little more before my presentation. You'll be in the room to watch and support me?"

Kai nodded. "And if you need me for anything, just say the word. Although I doubt it'll come to that."

"Only because you went over all the security stuff with me like fifty times. I'm just glad that's your job and not mine, because my eyes glazed over after the first go around." He grunted, and she laughed. "I'm teasing. But I do need to get ready. I'll see you in there?"

After kissing her again, he replied, "I'll be there. Good luck, love."

"Thanks."

Once Kai left her alone, Jane managed to fix her hair and smooth her dress. Ignoring how her face was paler than usual, she exited the toilet and went to the door separating the two rooms. She took one last fortifying breath before turning the knob and entering.

All seven leaders sat at a long table facing the front. Bram from Stonefire gave her a nod of encouragement, and Finn from Lochguard winked. Those two she knew would agree already.

Next, she spotted Rhydian Griffiths from Snowridge. And while the three scars—from dragon talons—on his face could be a little intimidating to strangers, Kai's mother, stepdad, and sister lived with the Welsh dragon clan and Jane had come to know Rhydian a little. He'd taken in an orphaned half-dragon-shifter boy—who'd turned out to be the nephew of his eventual human mate Delaney—and would be open to the idea. His clan was slow to welcome humans, though, because of lingering prejudices. Maybe half-dragon-shifter children would be easier to accept than full-blooded humans.

Next, she identified the two co-leaders from

Skyhunter, Asher King and Honoria Wakeham. Along with Northcastle's leader, Adrian Conroy, she knew them the least. Asher and Honoria had been busy rebuilding and healing their clan after the previous cruel leader. Still, they'd embraced a lot of changes suggested by Bram or Finn, so there was a chance they'd be on board with Jane's suggestion too.

Adrian, the Northcastle leader, sat next to the Skyhunter pair. Jane hadn't really talked to him since he'd taken over the clan, and she needed to rectify that when she had the chance.

Her gaze moved to the person sitting next to him— Glenlough's leader, Teagan O'Shea. The female Irish dragon leader smiled at her and gave a small nod. Teagan was mated to Aaron Caruso, who had been Kai's second-in-command before mating the Irish leader. No doubt Kai and Aaron had discussed the idea, and Aaron had then shared it with his mate. While not a guarantee of Teagan's support, it couldn't have hurt her case.

Kai stood behind them all, his gaze warm and full of support. Taking strength from her mate, Jane finally nodded at everyone and said, "Thank you all for agreeing to meet with me today, despite your busy schedule. However, the plan I'm proposing is important and will affect roughly a hundred lives. And not just any lives, but those of children.

"By now, we all know what went on inside the research facility Stonefire recently discovered. The one where they conducted experiments on dragon-shifters like they were mice or rats and not people. On top of that, many of their prisoners had been illegally purchased from half-dragon-shifter orphanages. And whilst the one that had been the main seller of children is no longer in operation, there are still roughly a hundred orphaned dragon children between the UK and Ireland. Children who should be raised amongst people who understand them. People who will help them embrace their inner dragons instead of teaching them to be ashamed, who can show them love instead of viewing them as a means to a paycheck, and who might want more children but struggle to have them."

She paused, deliberately not looking at Kai, and then added, "We should be taking in these children and giving them homes. The DDA has tentatively agreed to divide the monies given to the orphanages to the clans, to help settle them in. It has also agreed to establish safe places for any unwanted dragon children to be dropped off." She looked at each clan leader in turn. "But the DDA requires all of you to agree or they'll abandon the project. They granted leniency for the three other Irish dragon clans until things are more settled." She gestured at herself and then at the leaders. "It's up to us to lead the way. And I know you must have questions, so please ask them."

Rhydian from Snowridge frowned. "What if some of us can't take in as many as others? Things are improving on Snowridge, but some of the old timers are still prejudiced. I wouldn't want to take more than a few at first, to ease them into the idea."

Jane nodded. "Each clan has a different dynamic, a different feeling, and I'm sure we can work that out amongst everyone. I can't speak for the clan leaders, but I know enough from my mate to know that what seems impossible can become a reality with the right negotiations."

Teagan from Glenlough asked, "How will it work in Ireland? I don't know how many half-dragon orphans there are in my country, but I'm not sure my clan could take all of them, even if we wanted to."

Jane replied, "The British and Irish DDAs have agreed to allow Irish orphans to be fostered in the UK. At least, until the other Irish clans become more stable and can help."

It had been one of the hardest points to win over. However, Jane had been stubborn. And with Evie Moore-Llewellyn's help—Bram's mate and former DDA employee—they'd somehow convinced the two DDAs it was a good idea.

The evidence from Percy's former prison and her ties to the orphanage selling her had been compelling, though. And to say it was okay to allow children to be sold, tortured, and abused wasn't something any bureaucratic or political employee wanted hanging over them. Not even when it concerned dragon-shifters.

Jane remembered the time before Melanie Hall-MacLeod's book had been published, back when fears of the unknown had made most humans want nothing to do with dragon-shifters. Things had come quite far since then, and for the better.

Teagan said, "Then Glenlough would love to help, if that's the case."

Adrian from Northcastle spoke before anyone else. "What if they try to run away? Even if that one bloody awful orphanage has been shut down, the others might have filled the children's heads with rubbish about half-dragon children being unwanted."

Percy had been told that, to the point she'd been afraid of everyone on Stonefire in the beginning. Jane had looked into it the best she could. She replied, "It might happen, but if your Protectors are as talented as my mate, then you should be able to find them and reach out to Dr. Serafina Rossi or the newly trained dragon-shifter therapist, Dr. Torin Flynn. Both are willing to talk to any of the orphans, when needed, free of charge."

Dr. Rossi had been stretching herself thin recently, being the only dragon-shifter psychologist in the UK after Dr. Allonby from Snowridge had passed away. However, Dr. Flynn from Northcastle had completed his training and was helping to ease the burden.

Adrian grunted. "And if we need more help? I'm not trying to be difficult, but there have been a few runaways from most of our clans in the past. And some people simply don't want any help, let alone are willing to trust us."

He was right. Even Stonefire had dealt with some of its members running off to go into hiding, banding with other dragon-shifters who didn't like all the changes. Some had even attacked Lochguard at one point.

Jane said, "Hopefully, with the younger children, it will be easier. As for the older ones, all we can do is welcome them, show them how they're wanted, and try to give them the home they never had." She glanced around the room. "Many of us have seen how love can change a person for the better. Why would this be any different?"

Finn spoke up. "Aye, lass. Lochguard is willing to help."

Bram said, "And Stonefire too."

Rhydian grunted. "As long as we can start with a smaller group, Snowridge will help as well. My adopted son is half-human, and I couldn't imagine not taking him in. Not helping others like Rian would be wrong."

That meant she only had Northcastle and Skyhunter left to convince.

Not wanting to beat around the bush, she addressed Asher and Honoria. "What about Skyhunter?"

Honoria glanced at Asher—who was also her mate—and then answered, "We want to. But children require a lot of medical attention, and Skyhunter has struggled with only one doctor since the DDA recruited Dr. Harper for some project. Until we get another one, I'm not sure if we can say yes. We'd love to welcome orphans to Skyhunter, but I want to ensure we can take care of them properly."

This was something Jane hadn't realized in advance. Stonefire had so many doctors, she just assumed it was the same with most clans. Even Lochguard had two, plus a third one in training.

As she tried to think of a solution, Bram spoke up. "I would need to discuss it with Sid, Gregor, and Trahern, but if Trahern is willing, he might help you out until you can finish training your second doctor." Bram glanced at Rhydian. "As long as you don't mind. He is technically part of your clan."

Dr. Trahern Lewis was the Welsh dragon doctor

who had come to Stonefire a while ago to help with research. He was a bit odd, but extremely intelligent. Even if his bedside manner wasn't the greatest, he would do whatever it took to save a patient.

Rhydian shrugged. "He's been on Stonefire so long, I sort of think of him as one of yours now, aye? But Trahern needs to agree. The lad isn't the greatest with change and forcing him wouldn't help anyone."

Bram replied, "I'll talk to him."

Adrian from Northcastle jumped in. "We have a third doctor in training right now. I can't send another to help Skyhunter out yet, but it's a possibility when she finishes her training."

Hope bloomed in Jane's chest. Both from the offer from Bram, but also the one from Adrian. If the Northcastle leader was willing to lend a doctor when he could, then did it mean he was also on board to agree to her project? She asked, "Adrian, what about Northcastle?"

The Northern Irish dragon clan leader crossed his arms over his chest and stared at her. If he was trying to make her squirm, he'd be waiting a long, long time. If she could outlast Kai's stares and frowns, she could outlast anyone's.

Eventually, the tall dragon leader shrugged one shoulder. "I'm willing to try. But I do have one question, though. You were supposed to be the person in charge of this all, as a sort of point person, correct?"

"Yes," she said slowly, unsure of where this was going.

"Then what will happen when you have your baby? Who will be in charge then?"

She echoed, "Baby?"

What in the world was he talking about?

Her gaze shot to Kai. His eyes were full of love, his pupils flashing, and he nodded.

Jane looked down and placed a hand over her belly. When had this happened? Why hadn't Kai told her?

Would she be able to keep it to term, or would she lose it? She wasn't compatible with dragon-shifters, after all. And if she lost it, would she want to try again? Would Kai be disappointed in her? What if, what if, what if raced through her brain.

And as the questions whirred through her mind, she felt light-headed and the room tilted. Jane barely registered that she'd fallen and Kai had caught her before the world went black.

Chapter Six

B loody stupid Adrian Conroy, and his blurting out that Jane was pregnant. Kai had only noticed the change in her scent in the bathroom and had wanted to wait until after the meeting to share the news. He hadn't wanted to fuck up her pitch.

And then Conroy had done it.

Watching Jane's face shift from confusion to worry tore at his heart. Then he noticed her wobble, and he dashed up toward the front of the room, catching her right before she hit the ground.

As he stroked his mate's forehead, he growled out, "Call Dr. Sid."

Someone said they had, but he didn't pay attention to anything else said behind him. No, he didn't like his Janey pale and unconscious.

His dragon spoke up. *It's just shock.*

We don't know that. Given how she's conceived despite not being compatible means anything could happen.

Dr. Sid wouldn't give her anything dangerous.

Bram knelt next to Kai. "How is she?"

As he brushed hair from his mate's forehead, he replied, "I don't know. She's pale, Bram. And I don't like it."

Bram said, "I know it probably won't mean anything, but it happens with some pregnancies. Evie was sick and pale a lot when she carried Eleanor. Some babies just cause more trouble."

Finn knelt close by. "Aye, Arabella struggled with the triplets. At least our fourth one is being a wee bit better behaved."

Jane moaned and slowly blinked open her eyes. Kai never stopped caressing her cheek as he said, "Janey, are you okay?"

Her eyes eventually stayed open, and she raised a hand to rub her forehead. "I think so." She lowered her hand to point at him. "Why didn't you tell me?"

He didn't miss a beat. "I didn't know until right before the meeting. I thought it better to share the news after."

"Kai, you know how I hate to be in the dark about anything. You should've told me."

Before he could reply, Dr. Sid rushed into the room, a medical bag in her hand. "Let me through."

Bram and Finn stood, moving aside to allow Dr. Sid to kneel next to Jane. As soon as the doctor was settled, she glanced between them, a knowing look in her eyes. She could smell Kai's scent intertwined with Jane's, signaling she was pregnant.

The doctor motioned toward Jane. "Can you sit up on your own, Jane? If not, we can lie you down. Either way, I need room to work and your big, muscled mate is in the way."

His dragon growled. *She's our mate and carries our young. Of course we're going to protect her.*

Calm down. This is Sid.

His beast sniffed. *Still, Janey is ours.*

He sent soothing thoughts to his beast as Jane said, "I think I can sit up."

Kai helped her into a seated position. Even though he wanted to pull Jane close, he settled for holding her hand instead as the doctor asked questions and checked Jane over.

Once Dr. Sid finished, she looked at Jane. "I think being sick and emptying your stomach, combined with being pregnant and slightly stressed, caused your fainting. However, I'd like to get you to the surgery to draw some blood and run a few tests."

Jane's voice was low as she asked, "Should I be worried?"

Kai squeezed her hand in reassurance, but Jane's focus remained on Dr. Sid. The doctor answered calmly, "You know I don't like conjecture, especially with no data to base it upon. Let's just get you to the surgery and see what happens." The doctor shifted her gaze to Kai. "Can you carry her?"

"Of course."

Jane frowned. "Is that necessary?"

Kai and Dr. Sid said at the same time, "Yes."

Jane sighed and then mumbled, "So much for acing my presentation."

Kai lifted his mate and lowered his head to her ear. "You did well, Janey. All we need to do is talk to

Adrian, and I'm sure Bram and the others will do that. But never forget it was you and your determination that started it all."

She laid her head on his shoulder. "I know. Still, I don't like leaving things unfinished."

"I'll keep you updated, I promise. For now, your health is all that matters."

She fell silent, and Kai didn't mind. It wasn't strained. Besides, Jane looked even paler and dark circles had formed under her eyes.

He didn't like either.

Once they arrived at the surgery and to an examination room, he put Jane down and Dr. Sid immediately pointed toward the door. "Leave us. I'll call you when I'm done."

He grunted. "I won't leave my mate."

Dr. Sid didn't blink an eye. "Kai Sutherland, I will call in other Protectors to drag your arse out of the room, if needed. Don't be stubborn and just go. It won't be for long."

He debated whether to test the doctor's threats—Sid rarely made them unless she planned to carry them through—when Jane's voice garnered his attention. "It's okay, Kai. Let Dr. Sid do her job. The sooner you leave, the sooner you can come back."

Kai searched his mate's gaze and finally sighed. "The steel in your eyes tells me I won't win." He kissed her cheek. "But as soon as the doctor says she's done, I'm coming back in."

Jane squeezed his hand in hers. "I love you, Kai. Now, go."

He smiled, released his mate's hand, and went into

the hallway, where Dr. Innes stood. He gestured down the hallway. "Come, lad. Let's get out of the way and let Cassidy do her work. And whilst we wait, you can ask me any questions you might have."

Even though every step away from Jane felt wrong, Kai followed Dr. Innes into a small, private waiting room.

As the minutes ticked by, he only hoped it meant Dr. Sid was doing a thorough job and would have more ways to help them, if needed. Because Jane conceiving had been difficult, but he suspected it was only the beginning.

But regardless of what happened, he just wanted to hold Jane in his arms and take care of her.

Chapter Seven

J ane somehow managed to keep herself together as Dr. Sid drew blood and ran some tests. While a few of the results wouldn't be back until tomorrow, there were some they'd get right away.

Although the brief wait was bloody torture. So many scenarios ran through her head and most of them weren't good. After all, if she was barely pregnant and already fainting, what did that say about the rest of her pregnancy? If she could keep the baby, that was.

She missed Kai's calm, rational presence. While her dragonman felt things deeply and shared it with her, he always had a way of easing her runaway brain.

After nearly thirty minutes, Dr. Sid entered with Dr. McFarland from Lochguard. The two dragon women stood at the foot of her bed, and Jane blurted, "What did you find out?"

Dr. Sid spoke first. "You are indeed pregnant and most of your levels are normal. However, your body's white blood cell count is high, as if fighting against an infection. Probably because of your incompatibility with dragon-shifters."

Jane placed her hands on her stomach as tears pricked her eyes. "I'll lose the baby, won't I?"

It was crazy, as she'd only just learned of her pregnancy. And yet, after so many months of waiting and wanting, to have it snatched away so quickly made her want to hide under the covers and cry.

Dr. McFarland shook her head. "Not necessarily. Just like other humans who conceive dragon-shifter children, we're going to administer small doses of dragon's blood. More specifically, Kai's. The hope is that it will help your body accept the bairn, as well as protect you from complications."

Dr. Sid added, "You'll also need to take the fertility drugs you've been on as well. However, those things will be the easy part. The last recommendation will be the hardest for you."

Jane looked between the two doctors. "Which is?"

Dr. Sid replied, "You'll need to be on bedrest, maybe even for the entirety of your pregnancy."

"What?"

Dr. McFarland moved to sit beside her. "Aye, I know it's not anything someone wants to hear, let alone experience. But I had to endure many months of bedrest myself for my twin lads, and I'd do it again in a heartbeat to have my bairns."

Jane tried to process everything the doctors had said—more treatments, staying on the fertility drugs that often gave her headaches, and then nearly nine months of staying in bed.

And yet, just imagining Kai's face when he held

their baby for the first time made everything else pale in comparison. Not just for him, either, but for her, too. She wanted a little Kai running around, giving them trouble but also being as honorable as his or her father.

Although one thing did make her blurt, "Kai's going to drive me crazy with this news, won't he?"

Layla chuckled. "Aye, he will. My Chase isn't even a Protector, and he still hovered and worried over me constantly. But there are perks to it—you can ask for anything and your mate will get it, no matter how ridiculous it might be."

Worries still bounced around inside her head, so Jane looked at Dr. Sid and asked, "If I do all this, what's your best guess at me carrying to term?"

Dr. Sid's face softened. "I can't guarantee anything, as much as I want to. But if you give your permission to discuss your case with all the doctors gathered here, we can increase your chances of success, I'm sure of it. There are bound to be other things we can do to ensure you get to have your baby." Dr. Sid paused, and then added, "Although this will likely be your only one, Jane. Your body will go through a lot and try to fight against the pregnancy, and I wouldn't recommend going through it a second time."

Jane shook her head. "I don't care about more babies—there are plenty of children that need homes. But I just want one with Kai, to give him what he gave up when he picked me to be his mate."

Dr. McFarland took her hand. "Lass, he didn't give up anything. I've seen how he looks at you, and you are his world, Jane. If you're going to put your body through this, then ensure it's because you want a child too."

Jane nodded. "I do. And not just to annoy my brother's daughters."

Dr. Sid raised an eyebrow. "Nikki and Rafe only have one daughter so far."

Jane smiled. "I think they'll have two soon." She sobered. "But yes, I want to try and keep this baby. I'm aware my chances aren't good, but if I have to stay in bed the whole time, I will."

Dr. Sid bobbed her head. "Then we'll do all that we can to try and make it happen. You have more doctors than you will ever need for the next week, so there will always be someone on hand to help. And I can discuss this with them?" Jane nodded and the doctor continued, "Well, then we should probably have Gregor bring in Kai. We'll stay to explain it all and make sure he knows not to smother you while trying to take care of you."

The corner of Jane's mouth kicked up. "I'm pretty good at telling him to sod off, when needed."

Both doctors laughed, and Dr. McFarland said, "I don't doubt it, lass. Now, let's tell your mate everything and then you need to rest. You'll get a shot of dragon's blood today and then you'll stay the night, just to be safe, so we can monitor you and the bairn."

As Dr. Sid left to fetch Kai and Dr. McFarland wrote some notes on her chart, Jane picked at the sheet and took a few deep breaths. Kai was about to become extremely overbearing and overprotective, and she'd need her strength to tame it. Because she meant to start as they went on.

Although once the doctors finished telling Kai her situation, what to expect, and how he needed to listen to her, Kai lay down next to her on the small bed and pulled her close. He kissed the top of her head and said, "Dragon cuddles to make you feel better."

She laughed. "So this is what it took for you to freely offer them, huh?"

As she relaxed against her mate, he grunted. "Want to know a secret, Janey?"

She glanced up at Kai. "I thought we didn't keep secrets?"

"Usually, no. But I do have one."

"Which is?"

He whispered, "I fucking love dragon cuddles with my mate."

Jane laughed and hugged Kai closer. "I knew it the whole time."

And as they fell asleep together like that, Jane knew the coming days and months would be difficult. But as long as she had Kai, she could endure anything.

Chapter Eight

Adrian Conroy hadn't tried to be a bastard and make Jane Hartley faint. He'd simply had a question and assumed everyone else could smell her pregnancy.

But as Jane and her mate left with the doctor, Asher King came up to him and grunted. "Was that question really necessary?"

Adrian was several inches taller than Asher and glanced down to meet the Skyhunter leader's eyes. "What? It's a legitimate concern. She clearly has a passion, but who else will be working with her? It's no different than asking who would be in charge when a clan leader's mate went into labor."

Finn Stewart walked up to them and said, "Are you sure about that, Conroy? Or are you just looking for an excuse not to join in?"

Part of him was, in fact, doing exactly that. But not because it would be difficult to convince older dragon-shifters to take in a few orphans, especially if they were from Ireland. No, he had another big reason, having to do with a certain female.

His dragon spoke up. *It's highly unlikely she will make the visits.*

You say that, but you know she conducts clan check-ins for transfers and human mates.

The "she" in question was Elsie Day—the human female he'd once kissed, started a frenzy, and then had been torn away from to suffer alone. Even if the true mate pull faded with time, Adrian didn't want to risk it. Especially since he'd only become clan leader recently, and he still had a lot to prove.

Not that he'd tell the other clan leaders about that. He might be getting to know them and trying to trust them, but he wasn't about to offer up weaknesses freely, for them to dangle over him.

His dragon sighed. *Stop being so distrustful and wary.*

Given our past, you should know it's not that easy.

Before his dragon could reply, Finn cleared his throat, garnering his attention. The Scottish leader said, "If Jane or Kai can't be reached, Evie Marshall and Ivy Passmore are working to help her."

He grunted. "You want the former Dragon Knight female in charge of this?"

While the group known as the Dragon Knights had been disbanded, they'd caused pain, trouble, and death for dragon-shifters for years.

Bram joined their group, with Rhydian at his side. Bram said, "Aye, I do trust her. Ivy's been trying to make up for hurting our kind for a long time now."

Adrian wished it was that easy for him. While the instances of dragons being hunted and captured were declining in England and Scotland, it wasn't the same case in Northern Ireland. Between the chaos in the three clans in the Republic of Ireland and the struggle for the Irish and UK Department of Dragon Affairs to work together, dragon hunters were flourishing on the Isle of Ireland. But especially near Belfast, which wasn't far from Adrian's clan.

In fact, he was worried about bringing anyone new onto Northcastle until he managed to get the dragon hunter problem under control.

Honoria Wakeham, the other Skyhunter leader, joined their group with Teagan O'Shea, the Glenlough leader and probably the dragon-shifter in the group he knew the best. Honoria said, "Surely there's a way we can iron this out, Adrian. You can do like Snowridge and start small."

He glanced at Teagan, who understood his concerns without him saying a word. She gestured with her head for them to go outside. "Let's chat for a moment, aye?" She looked at the rest of the clan leaders. "We won't be long."

Rhydian grunted. "Five minutes and then we'll find you. We need to get this sorted so I can check on my mate and children."

Teagan smiled. "Of course." She pushed against Adrian's back. "Come on."

They exited the hall and went into a side room. As soon as the door closed, Teagan turned on him and crossed her arms over her chest. Raising one dark eyebrow, she asked, "Why don't you just ask them for help? That's the whole point of these meetings, Adrian. I vowed I wouldn't share your clan troubles without your permission—as long as it doesn't hurt my clan—but trying to tackle it on your own won't help anyone."

He grunted. "I only took over the leadership this year, and I need to show I can handle it. Besides, you're the female who hid her true identity for years, out of fear that other clans would attack since you're female. So I'm not sure you have a leg to stand on."

Teagan narrowed her eyes. "Don't alienate your best ally, Adrian. You might be a good Protector and know how to talk to your clan members, but you're shite when it comes to relying on others. Eventually, that will bring you down, if you're not careful."

His dragon spoke up. *Why are you making her angry?*

Ignoring his beast, he replied, "How about this compromise—I'll agree to take one or two children at first, and then attempt to tackle my dragon hunter problem by myself. If after six months I can't contain them, I'll reach out to everyone and ask for their help."

Teagan shook her head. "I still don't like it. It's not like the old days, aye? We aren't feuding and trying to take each other down."

"Perhaps. But seeing as a few Irish clan leaders were out to kill you not too long ago, I think you'd want to be cautious."

She stared at him and finally sighed. "They say the Conroys are stubborn bastards, and you're just proving the point."

And they held grudges. Not that he'd add that detail.

Adrian said, "I know Lochguard and Stonefire have an extremely close relationship, but despite Northcastle's former leader mating your mother, we aren't quite to that place, Teagan. I'm trying, but it'll take time. Some of my clan members are still upset about your brother avoiding and rejecting Georgiana Todd."

Teagan sighed. "That again? Killian and Georgiana would've made each other miserable."

"Perhaps. But there are still some dragon-shifters who believe we should only be with our true mates or no one at all."

"A load of rubbish, if I'd ever heard it."

Considering Teagan had mated Aaron Caruso, who wasn't her true mate, he understood her sentiment.

"Maybe. But just like it's taking time for many to accept human males mating female dragon-shifters, it's the same inside Northcastle about mating someone not your true mate. Just give me six months to work on this stuff, and then we'll talk again about it."

Teagan eyed him a beat, her pupils flashing to slits and back, and then said, "Fine. But only as long as the problem doesn't start to spiral out of control. Because if it starts to affect more than just Northcastle, I won't hold back, aye?"

She put out her hand to shake, and Adrian took it. "Of course."

Teagan released his hand. "Well, then let's tell them you'll foster a few orphans. The sooner we can get the wee ones homes with their kind, the better. I shudder to think of them being raised as mostly human and being told to contain their dragons as much as possible."

Percy had shared her story with all the clan leaders, to let them know exactly what had been happening to some of the orphaned dragon-shifter children. Not long after their dragons appeared, they'd often been silenced and taught to act more as if they were human.

The female's story had been sobering, to say the least.

Adrian gestured toward the door. "Let's go tell the others my answer."

As he followed Teagan into the room, he only hoped he could protect any children sent to Northcastle —both from enemies and possibly even some of his own clan members.

His dragon spoke up. *Anyone who hurts them, or tries to make them feel unwelcome, will be dealt with.*

Yes, but he had to decide if banishment would be the best choice. Lochguard had done that, and now there was a clan-less group of dragons hiding somewhere, waiting to pounce.

Regardless, Adrian would find a solution. After all, he'd wanted to be clan leader to effect change. This was just one more thing he'd add to his list to handle.

Chapter Nine

K ai watched his mate, asleep on his chest, and he tried to come to terms with everything that had happened. Part of him was overjoyed at the fact she'd finally conceived. And yet, a larger part of him was worried. There were so many fucking risks.

His dragon spoke up. *Jane's choice is to try and have the baby. If Dr. Sid says it's too dangerous, no doubt Janey will listen.*

He wanted to believe that. But he also knew that Jane viewed having his baby as a sort of way to prove they were meant to be together. Even after everything that had happened, his mate still doubted him. And it stung a little.

His dragon grunted, but Jane stirred a little, meaning she'd wake up soon. His beast added quickly, *I don't think it's doubt, but more that she wants a family.*

I'd already planned on suggesting to her that we should adopt one of the orphans.

Yes, but with me and not with her. You should tell her.

Jane's eyes fluttered open, and she blinked a few times before meeting his gaze. She smiled. "Morning."

He kissed her. "How do you feel, love?"

"Better. Well, at least lying down. We'll have to see what happens once I eat and try to move around."

He caressed her cheek with the back of his knuckles. "Whatever you need, just ask for it, Janey."

She adjusted so that she sat up, facing him. For a few beats, she merely stared at him, as if trying to read his expression. Finally she said, "You don't seem as happy as I thought you'd be, Kai. Why?"

Taking her hand in his, he replied, "I am happy, but also worried." He brought her hand to his mouth and kissed the back of it. "You're my everything, Janey. I wish you'd accept that."

She bit her bottom lip and then sighed. "I know, Kai. I think at first, trying to have a baby was a way to prove we were supposed to be together. I know you rejected Maggie, and not even her kiss affects your dragon any longer. But—"

"No fucking buts." He moved closer, until their faces weren't more than a few inches apart. "You're mine, Jane. Mine. And if you want a child, we can adopt one. Hell, we can adopt five, if you so wish." He cupped her cheek and caressed it with his thumb. "You don't have to risk your life to prove anything."

She placed her hand over his. "I know. But I want to try, Kai. I'll probably drive you mad when I'm on bedrest. I'll be grumpy, and short-tempered, and I'll get bored easily. But despite the risks, I want to at least try. I trust Dr. Sid."

"As long as you promise me that if she says your life is in danger, you'll listen."

She nodded. "I will. I can be stubborn, which will help in the coming months, but not to the point I want to die from it."

A rush of relief coursed through him. "Good. Because I won't survive without you, Janey. I don't want to."

She moved until she sat in Kai's lap and looped her arms around his neck. "Well, at least maybe now you understand a little about how I feel whenever you rush into a dangerous job." He grunted, but she continued before he could say anything. "But I know protecting the clan is part of who you are, and I wouldn't change it. Still, it's fucking terrifying." She kissed his lips gently. "And just as you always tell me you'd move heaven and earth to come back to me, I'm going to do the same to stay right here by your side. Even if it means I have to make a hard decision."

Kai brushed the hair from his mate's face. "The shot of my dragon's blood has already improved your coloring, and I suspect Dr. Sid and her doctor group will suggest other things to help. So let's hope it doesn't come to that."

She smiled at him. "Thank you for at least allowing me to try, even with some risk."

"As if I could deny you anything."

A playful glint entered her eyes. "So once I've had the baby and am well again, does that mean I can go to Ireland and interview the new clan leaders?"

He raised an eyebrow. "We'll see. It would need to

be by the book, and I would have to accompany you. But I'll at least consider it."

She grinned at him, making her even more beautiful. "So fainting and being pregnant is all it took?"

He drawled, "It's almost as if you planned all of this in advance."

She laughed. "No. Although I plan to use this situation to my advantage as much as possible."

Bringing her closer, until she pressed more fully against his body, he murmured, "Try, love. But it's no guarantee it will always work."

And as Jane went through some ridiculous propositions—such as finally trying to ride his dragon form in a saddle some day despite her paralyzing fear of heights—he teased and cuddled and merely held his mate.

The times ahead were going to be tough, but he could face it with her. The hard part was waiting to hear how else the doctors might be able to help Jane.

Since all he could do was wait, Kai gave his mate plenty of dragon cuddles and merely reveled in holding his female close, where she belonged.

Chapter Ten

The next day, Sid sat in the biggest conference room on Stonefire and waited for the other dragon doctors to arrive.

Helping Jane had delayed the meeting by a day. But in a way, the delay had been a good thing. Because now she had even more blood test results from the human female. Some were better than she thought, but some not so much.

The fertility pills mixed with dragon-shifter hormones would help, as would shots of dragon's blood. However, Sid was worried about Jane's kidneys. According to the test results, they were drawing nearer and nearer to dangerous levels.

Her, Gregor, Trahern, and Dr. Emily Davies—the Welsh human doctor who'd been working on Stonefire—had all brainstormed about what to do to address the issue. However, they were too close to the situation and desperately needed some fresh eyes.

Sid refused to give up now. Despite everyone saying

it couldn't be done, she'd drastically improved survival rates for humans having dragon-shifter children. Next, she wanted to give any couple the chance to have a child whether the human's DNA was compatible with dragon-shifters or not. Because one day, Sid hoped for more acceptance by humans, maybe to the point dragon-shifters wouldn't be restricted to living in clans.

Her dragon sighed. *You don't dream small, do you?*

Never. And if you don't know that by now, then I'm not sure what I can do.

Although, as soon as she said it, Sid wished she could take it back. Her dragon had been absent for years and years because of a silent dragon drug overdose. Once Gregor's kiss had awakened her beast and kicked off a mate-claim frenzy, they'd had to work on their relationship and play catch up.

Her beast said softly, *It's okay. And I do know you fairly well. But I like to tease more than you.*

Just so you can keep up with Gregor's dragon.

Maybe.

Sid smiled at memories of their dragons coming out to play just as the door opened and Dr. Maelon Perry from Snowridge walked in, with Dr. Cahir Silver from Northcastle close on his heels. She nodded at the two males. "Maelon, Cahir. Are the others coming?"

Maelon smiled. "Yes. Scarlett wanted to look something up last minute, and Ronan and Daniel were just finishing up breakfast." He glanced around the room. "Are the other Stonefire doctors coming?"

Sid replied, "Trahern is, yes. But Gregor is at the surgery so he can watch over the patients, and I'll catch him up later at whatever happens in our meeting." Sid gestured toward the chairs. "Please, sit down. We can get started as soon as the others arrive."

They chatted over a few cases until the other doctors arrived: Dr. Scarlett Turner from Skyhunter, Dr. Daniel Keith from the Scottish splinter clan of Seahaven, Dr. Layla McFarland from Lochguard, Dr. Ronan O'Brien from Glenlough, and Dr. Trahern Lewis, who worked with Sid and Gregor on Stonefire. Sid had tried to convince Dr. Emily Davies to come, but she'd insisted it was a meeting for dragon doctors and she was human.

Once everyone was seated, Sid didn't waste time. "Thank you all for coming. I know we've had many meetings via video conferences, but it's nice to see each other in person. And whilst we have a number of things to discuss, I propose we go over the information I sent last night first."

Sid had sent emails to all the doctors, with details about Jane's case. Given the small miracle of Jane being able to conceive a dragon-shifter's child, Sid wanted to be proactive and give mother and baby the best chance.

Scarlett from Skyhunter spoke first. "There hasn't been much time, but there are a few things I came up with. Given Skyhunter's recent past—which also reduced our birth rates further, due to the former leader's control over matings and pregnancies—helping any and all females who want to conceive and carry to term has become one of my top priorities. During my research, I came across a former doctor's journal, one that is dated from over a hundred and fifty years ago."

Sid leaned forward. Finding any sort of old dragon-shifter medical records was rare. Many of the books had been destroyed over the years, sometimes at the DDA's command. She asked, "Did it have anything useful inside?"

The female doctor nodded. "Yes. It's mostly a record of medicinal plants in Sussex and their uses. There were also some early chemistry formulas and experiment notes. After losing his sister to childbirth, a doctor named John Greystone concentrated on helping pregnant females. There are some new methods I haven't seen before. Or, rather, were forgotten. We might be able to try testing if any of the doctor's suggestions have merit." She glanced at Trahern. "Research is more your strength than mine. Would you be willing to go over his formulas and test any that might help?"

Trahern nodded. "Send me the information."

Sid jumped in again. "Maybe send the information to us all?"

Scarlett was a few years younger than Sid, with a healed scar on her cheek. The female had been nearly done with her doctor's training when she'd refused to follow the former Skyhunter leader's order to use imprisoned clan members as test subjects. While Sid knew the female had paid the price herself by being tossed into a jail cell, she didn't know the details about what other horrors she must've endured. However, Sid was immensely glad Scarlett hadn't lost her love of medicine and had finished her training recently.

The Skyhunter doctor nodded. "No worries, I'll send it to everyone, and I hope it's just the beginning. You see, I found the journal in a secret alcove, and I'm trying to see if there are any more hidden caches around the clan. If I find more information, I'll let you know."

Maelon from Snowridge spoke up. "Dr. Hughes is still testing things in his retirement. If I can share the details of this human female patient with him, it might help."

Dr. Hughes had shared a little-known remedy in the past to help some drugged dragon-shifters, and Sid trusted him. She said, "Sure. I do wish he could've come too."

Maelon smiled. "He says he's too old to fly for so long. But he'll be willing to help."

Cahir from Northcastle spoke next. "Whilst my speciality isn't gynecology, I have experience with kidney disease and failure. I noticed her levels are high, so if I can take a vial of Jane's blood back with me, I can try a few things to see if it helps bring them down."

Sid nodded, and Ronan from Glenlough immediately chimed in next. "And whilst her glucose levels are fine for now, they should be monitored closely. If her pancreas starts failing, I might be able to help there."

As Sid looked at each of the doctors in the room, a mixture of pride and accomplishment rushed through her. She'd worked so bloody hard to achieve exactly this —a meeting of dragon doctors from different clans, who could all contribute something different to give a patient their best chance.

She wished Gregor was here too, to share this moment.

Her dragon spoke up. *We have all week to share these*

meetings with him. But it doesn't matter—he's already told us how proud he is of us.

It was true. Sid could never have found a better, supportive mate than Gregor Innes.

Not wanting emotion to tumble out, she cleared her throat, took a few deep breaths, and said to the room, "Thank you, everyone. The fact you want to help one of my clan members means the world to me."

Layla from Lochguard smiled at her. "Aye, of course, Sid. I know you'd do the same for us, if we asked."

Sid nodded. "Any time."

As they finished up details concerning Jane's case, they moved on to other business. And by the end of the meeting, Sid still had trouble believing it wasn't all a dream. When she'd been a new doctor, she never could've imagined so many doctors sharing their thoughts and ideas. For decades—probably longer— each clan had viewed their medical knowledge as a secret to keep from other clans. It'd never made sense to her, though. Human doctors shared information, released research papers, and even had conferences.

While she hadn't quite reached that level yet, this meeting of UK and Irish doctors was just the beginning. One day she would have a much wider net, with as much cooperation as the humans did.

Her dragon spoke up. *We'll do it. But make sure to have time for Gregor and Wyatt.*

I know, dragon. Besides, Gregor would never let me work as much as I had before mating him, when work was the only thing to keep me going.

Good thing too. Now, let's find him.

Knowing her beast, she replied, *None of* that *until later.*

Her beast sniffed. *We can kiss our mate, surely.*

But where?

Her dragon laughed. *His cock, to start.*

Sid battled a smile, but couldn't scold her dragon. After all, she wanted to celebrate with Gregor. Not only because of the success of the meeting, but also because he hadn't blinked an eye when she'd asked him to keep an eye on the patients instead of attending.

She had the handsomest, cleverest, most supportive mate a female could ask for.

She replied to her dragon, *Maybe we'll kiss him after all.*

Starting with his cock?

We'll see, dragon, we'll see.

Once she reached home and discovered that Wyatt was with Harris, Sid kissed her mate. First on the mouth, and then every last inch she could.

Chapter Eleven

Nikola "Nikki" Gray-Hartley frowned down at her abdomen as pain rippled through her. She was good at hiding emotions when needed—it came with the territory of being a Protector—but she felt her mate's eyes on her. And if there was one person who could detect the slightest change in her expression, it was Rafe Hartley.

Most of the time, she loved how bloody observant he was. But right now, it was going to make him a huge pain in her arse.

Her dragon laughed. *And he hasn't been one for the entire pregnancy?*

She mentally sighed. *Don't remind me, dragon.*

He was at her side instantly. "What's wrong, Nikki?" He placed a hand on her belly, but the possible contraction had stopped, thank goodness. He asked, "Is the baby telling you to take a break?"

She rolled her eyes. "How in the world did I end up as the stern parent? Louisa already has you wrapped around her little finger. This one isn't even born yet, and they're the same way."

His green-eyed gaze met hers, and she softened at the true concern she saw there.

Her dragon spoke up. *He's just worried. Rafe doesn't like to be out of control, and he can't control anything when it comes to the baby.*

I know. It's still bloody irritating at times, though.

Her dragon snorted. *We poke back at him just as much, so it's kind of fun.*

You would say that.

Rafe cupped her cheek. "Talk to me, Nikki. Because if you're hiding contractions from me to try and do your job, then I'm going to bloody scoop you up and carry you to the surgery, no matter how much you shout at me."

She raised an eyebrow. "I may be pregnant, but I can still shift into a dragon. You won't be able to carry me then."

"You can shift, but you can't fly, per the doctor's orders. And since you currently waddle in your dragon form, you won't get far."

She stuck her tongue out at him. "You're supposed to be nice to me."

Humor danced in his eyes. "Nice would be boring. I tried that in the beginning when you were pregnant with Louisa and you threatened to kick my arse to the curb unless I treated you like normal."

"Maybe," she grumbled. "But I feel as big as a whale, so maybe don't say I waddle."

Rafe leaned down and kissed her gently. "I showed

you this morning how fucking beautiful you are to me, love."

He had. Twice.

Nikki cleared her throat, wanting to tease him back. "I think you're just having sex with me as much as possible because of the oncoming dry spell."

Moving his hand from her belly to her arse, he pressed her up against him. Nikki never tired of Rafe's hard, hot body against hers, even when he had to lean awkwardly around her bloody big belly to do it. He couldn't quite press his chest against hers, though. And she couldn't wait until she stopped growing a person inside of her and could simply revel in her mate's arms.

He whispered, "I will always want to fuck you as much as possible, Nikola Hartley-Gray. Because you're mine, and I never want you to forget it."

Nikki shivered, in a good way. "Rafe."

Her mate tilted her head up toward his. "Nikki."

Just as he moved to kiss her, a gushing wetness rushed between her legs. "Bloody hell."

Her water had just broke.

Rafe, ever the soldier, jumped into action. He scooped her into his arms and rushed up the stairs to the bathroom. "Let's get you changed, and then I'll take you to the surgery."

She sighed. "It could be hours yet, Rafe. After all, it took Louisa forever to be born."

He grunted. "You're still going. And don't fight me on this, Nikki, because you won't win."

As pain rippled across her abdomen, she leaned her head on Rafe's shoulder and tried to breathe. The contraction had just finally passed when Rafe set her on her feet, steadying her with his hands on her hips. His gaze searched hers. "All right, love?"

"Maybe going to the surgery isn't such a bad idea. They do say the second baby usually comes quicker."

"Then let's get to work."

Rafe didn't waste time stripping them both, using a washcloth to clean her up, and then helping her dress. Considering she'd had another contraction during the short time, Nikki was fairly certain their baby wanted to come out and say hello. And soon.

By the time Rafe had her in his arms again, the contractions were too bloody close together. "Rafe, hurry. I don't want to have my baby on the footpath."

He started to run. "I thought you were the stern parent? Tell our second child to wait."

Nikki laughed. "As if that will work."

He winked at her before looking back to where he was going. "It's worth a shot."

They reached the surgery just as another contraction hit. She barely registered Rafe talking to a nurse and then Dr. Innes before her mate carried them to a room.

Once he laid her down, Dr. Innes listened to her heartbeat and then the baby's. After gently prodding and pushing her belly to determine the baby's position, he said, "Do you want Rafe to help you change or Ginny?"

Ginny was one of the nurses on Stonefire. And while Nikki usually loved the tough, stubborn nurse, right now, she just wanted her mate. "Rafe."

Dr. Innes nodded. "Aye, then I'll be back in five minutes to check on you and see how far along you are." He pinned his gaze on Rafe. "And maybe this time, you could avoid calling me a pain-loving bastard when it comes time to deliver your child?"

Rafe almost looked sheepish, no doubt remembering the litany of curses he'd thrown at the doctor when Louisa had been born. "I'll try."

Shaking his head, Dr. Innes left and Rafe helped Nikki change into a hospital gown. Once she was settled on the bed, Rafe took her hand and kissed the back of it. "There went my hopes of a last-minute tumble in the sheets with my mate."

He sighed dramatically, and she laughed. But a contraction hit at the same time and she groaned. She clutched Rafe's hand, but her mate never said a word despite the fact he was human and Nikki was far stronger than him.

Her dragon said softly, *We'd never hurt him. Well, unless he deserves it.*

Nikki nearly laughed again, but somehow held it back. And once the pain stopped, she said to her human, "Don't make me laugh right now, Rafe. Your spawn is trying to make a memorable appearance and seems to be in a hurry."

He brushed hair from her forehead and then kissed it. "Let me guess—the child is my spawn until he or she is born, and then they'll become yours until they cause trouble again?"

She smiled. "I've taught you well."

Rafe chuckled. "Somewhat."

The doctor returned, checked Nikki, and "The wee one is eager to come out and say hello. It won't be long now, lass."

Nikki nodded, grateful for Rafe's hand in hers. She was both eager and anxious to become a mum again.

Her dragon spoke up, *Everything will be fine. Our dad and stepmum love watching their grandchild, and will love having another one to spoil.*

It's the spoiling part I worry about.

As another contraction came, she clenched her jaw and tried to breathe. But it didn't help as much as she liked. And by the end of it, Nikki felt as if she'd just flown hundreds of miles in her dragon form, with no energy left.

Rafe kissed her forehead and murmured, "Do you want me to sit behind you, and you can brace against me?"

It had been the only position to help the last time, and tears pricked her eyes that Rafe remembered. "Yes, love. Please."

His lips twitched. "I love it when you beg."

She narrowed his eyes, and Rafe laughed.

It took some doing, but Rafe managed to sit behind her, and she sat between his legs, her back to his chest and him holding each of her hands with one of her own. Rafe nuzzled her cheek. "You're one of the strongest people I know, Nikki. You can do this."

His words were exactly what she needed to hear. Especially since in the next fifteen minutes, Baby Number Two was ready to greet the world and Nikki had to push another little dragon-shifter out of her body, screaming as she did so.

RAFE HARTLEY HATED how his mate was in pain and that he could do fuck all to help her beyond murmur encouragements and let her squeeze his hands to the point she might bruise his bones.

But he couldn't—wouldn't—complain. Despite Nikki's determination to act as if nothing was different during pregnancy, she struggled at times. It'd fucking killed him to watch her be sick or need a nap to make it through the day. Even if they'd both wanted another child, he wasn't sure he'd ever ask her to do this again.

When Dr. Innes finally said it was time to deliver the baby, Nikki was sweaty and grumpy. More than once, she suggested cutting off Rafe's balls to make sure this never happened again. And as she cried out and even screamed, he'd nearly agreed with her.

However, once their baby started coming, the delivery went quickly. Soon Rafe heard a baby's cry and Dr. Innes lifted the red, angry baby into the air and said, "You have another daughter."

Maybe later he'd think about how rare that was, to have two daughters in a row for any dragon-shifter. But right now, all he did was stare at the little half-dragon baby he'd helped to make and kissed his mate's cheek. "She's so bloody beautiful, Nikki. Just like her mum."

Nikki gave a tired laugh. "She's red, splotchy, and wrinkly. I'm not sure that's a compliment."

"Hush. For once, just agree with me."

It was a sign of just how tired Nikki was that she sighed and muttered, "Fine." She held out her arms. "Can I hold her?"

Dr. Innes had already cut the umbilical cord and, with the help of Nurse Ginny, had wrapped their daughter in a soft green blanket. He walked up and placed the baby in Nikki's arms, and Rafe wrapped his own around his mate's.

For a second, all he could do was stare and marvel at where his life had ended up. He was a father of two, with the most amazing, beautiful, and clever mate. "I love you, Nikki." He kissed her cheek. "And hello, Phoebe. Daddy loves you already, too."

The baby stopped crying and merely wriggled her nose, as if not liking her name.

Nikki adjusted the blanket around their daughter. "I told you, Rafe, that your name was rubbish."

"I thought it was rather brilliant. Try yours, then, and see how she reacts."

Nikki whispered, "How about Lucy? Isn't that so much better?" Their daughter merely moved a fist, and Nikki added, "That's a yes."

"How the bloody hell is that a yes?"

Nikki never took her eyes from their daughter. "It was like a fist in the air for success. She likes it."

Rafe tried it out. "So it's to be Lucy, then?"

Again, their daughter moved a fist.

Rafe sighed and then laughed. "Fine. It seems like this daughter is going to be a mummy's girl then."

Nikki leaned down and kissed Lucy's forehead. "Good. Now the three of you won't team up against me —the odds will be even."

Rafe gently traced a finger over his daughter's cheek. "I like that. It'll make future family competitions more interesting. Our daughters will be the fastest, most devious pair on all of Stonefire, if I can help it."

"If I leave it up to you, they'll be secret agents by the time they're sixteen," Nikki drawled.

Rafe smiled. "Maybe."

As he placed his cheek against Nikki's and merely stared down at little Lucy, Rafe took the time to memorize the moment. While it wouldn't be perfect until he had all three of his girls together, he was a fucking lucky and happy bastard right now.

Dr. Innes cleared his throat. "Nurse Ginny needs to check over the bairn and I need to finish up with Nikki. Did you want to wait at the back of the room with your daughter?"

As Ginny took Lucy, Nikki slumped against him and Rafe knew his mate needed him right now. "I'll stay right here, until Nikki and I can be with Lucy together."

Nikki melted more against him and whispered, "I love you."

"I love you too, Nikola."

Once Nikki had delivered the afterbirth and Lucy was back in Nikki's arms, Rafe didn't know how long they stayed together, staring at the new arrival, until a knock sounded. Immediately after, his sister walked inside. Jane looked pale, and Kai hovered at her side. Rafe had heard about Jane's fainting the day before and was torn between jumping up to check on his little sister and staying where he was.

Jane reached the bedside and put up a hand. "I'm fine, Rafe. I'm well enough to meet my new niece." She put out her hands. "Can I hold her?"

Kai grunted. "Are you strong enough?"

Jane rolled her eyes, but ignored her mate to wiggle her fingers toward them, wanting to hold Lucy.

Nikki helped to move their daughter to Jane's hands and shared her name. Once his sister had Lucy in her arms, she tickled her cheek and said, "Hello, little one. I'm your fun Auntie Jane. I knew you'd be a girl, and I hope you give your father hell."

She looked up at Rafe and grinned. Given how his sister had spent the night at the surgery, he decided to be a little nicer to her. But only a little. "She's already a mummy's girl, so she'll probably give me hell. Nikki's sure to give her lessons on how to push all my buttons."

Nikki rightly smacked his hand, which was wrapped around her middle. "For that, now I'll give both our daughters lessons."

Jane looked back at Lucy. "She's smaller than Louisa. If she's lucky, she might miss out on the super tall Hartley genes."

Kai was at her side, his arm around Jane's waist. "I rather liked the super tall Hartley genes."

As Jane shared a tender glance with her mate, Rafe resisted a smile. Sometimes Kai was a fucking annoying bastard, but he made Jane happy and that was all that mattered to Rafe.

Rafe kissed Nikki's cheek. "I like how Nikki's shorter than me. There can be advantages in combat for shorter statures, too. And I'll make sure Lucy learns them all. No one will want to mess with my daughters."

Nikki sighed. "Could we discuss combat training later? You know, maybe once she's learned how to walk?"

He grunted, wanting to needle his mate a little. "You can never start too early."

Kai nodded. "I agree. We should start a children's self-defense club."

Jane raised an eyebrow. "Only you two would think up that idea whilst Nikki has barely delivered her baby."

Nikki laughed. "It's very Kai and Rafe, though."

Rafe scowled and mentally swore as Kai did the same.

Before anyone could say anything else, Nikki's dad, Hector, and stepmother, Delphine, entered, carrying Louisa. She had her thumb in her mouth, her brown eyes wide, as she stared at Nikki and Rafe. She said around her thumb, "Baby?"

Jane moved toward Louisa and held up Lucy. "You have a little sister, Lou-lou."

Louisa looked down at the bundle and frowned, looking more like Nikki than Rafe had ever seen before. His daughter said, "She small."

Nikki laughed. "Yes, darling, she is. But you were small too. Now you have to be her big sister and teach her everything."

Jane moved back toward the bed and returned Lucy to Nikki's arms. As soon as Jane smiled at them both, Nikki's dad came forward, still carrying Louisa. Hector helped Louisa to sit beside Nikki on the bed. Once he had, he kissed Nikki's cheek and said, "She's beautiful, Nikki."

Delphine had walked to the opposite side and took Lucy's little hand in hers. "She is. Although I think she looks more like Rafe than Louisa ever did at this age."

Since both of their daughters had dark, nearly black hair, he muttered, "How the bloody hell can you tell that?"

Nikki leaned against him and replied to her stepmother, "It's the nose, I think. I hope she ends up with green eyes."

Rafe said, "I'm rather partial to brown, like her mother's."

Nikki shook her head. "This will soon devolve into some sort of ridiculous bet, and I'm too tired to do that right now."

He kissed Nikki's cheek again and reached to take Louisa's hand. She looked from the baby to Rafe and held out her other arm. "Daddy, up?"

Rafe was torn since his mate needed him too, but Nikki patted his arm. "I'll be fine, Rafe. Truly."

He nodded at Louisa. "All right, sweetheart, Daddy's coming."

Hector picked up Louisa again so Rafe could slowly maneuver out from behind Nikki. With Delphine's help, Nikki moved back to lay on the pillows with Lucy still in her arms.

Rafe swooped Louisa up and gently tossed her into the air to make her giggle. Then he settled her against his chest and sat down on the bed, next to Nikki. With all of his girls there, Rafe felt an overwhelming sense of love and protectiveness. It was still strange to think that one spur-of-the-moment kiss had started all of this. And yet, he was glad it had worked out. Because he wouldn't change a thing, not for all the money in the world.

Chapter Twelve

Kaylee MacDonald's stomach roiled, and she did her best to keep her breakfast down. She really shouldn't have come down to Stonefire, given her secret, and yet she hadn't been able to say no to Finn's request to help out. Her clan duties were watching over the children, including the clan leader's triplets, and she had no real reason to refuse.

Well, there was a reason, but one she didn't know what the hell to do about.

As the overpowering vanilla scent she'd applied hit her nose, she hoped it was enough. Because she knew by now that if a woman was pregnant with a dragon-shifter's child, her scent would be intertwined with the guy in question, and she didn't want anyone knowing her secret. Since she didn't know the father's identity, she couldn't even share the news with him.

Why she'd ever thought attending a clandestine, masked dragon-shifter party in the wilds of Scotland had been a good idea, she didn't know. But at the time,

Kaylee had been frustrated that no one on Lochguard had taken notice of her—or if they had, they hadn't sparked any attraction for her—and she'd wanted some sort of anonymous, no-strings-attached sex with a hot dragonman.

Yes, he'd worn a condom. However, apparently that hadn't been enough. She really should've listened to her sister's advice about taking dragon-shifter approved birth control before jumping between the sheets with one. Especially since all a man had to do was look at a MacDonald woman and she'd end up pregnant.

She resisted a sigh. Too little, too late to heed Gina's advice now.

Little Annabel MacLeod rushed up to her, covered in mud, and pointed behind her. "Jack's throwing mud at everyone. You need to stop him."

Given what Kaylee knew of the twins, Annabel had probably started it. Still, she took a deep breath to calm her stomach and gestured for the little girl to lead her. "Okay, bring me to where you all were playing and we'll go from there."

Kaylee smiled over at Dawn Whitby-Chadwick, who was also helping to watch the kids, and motioned with her head to say she was checking something out. The other human woman nodded, and Kaylee took Annabel's hand to keep her from running off—it was common knowledge that Annabel MacLeod liked to run off if something interesting caught her eye.

They approached an area where Jack MacLeod, Rhys James, and Murray Moore-Llewellyn were all huddled together and hiding something from everyone.

Rhys was the oldest in the group, and he looked up to see Annabel and narrowed his eyes. "You snitched!"

Annabel stood tall. "You're not playing fair."

"Then you shouldn't have thrown the first mud ball."

"I did not."

Murray nodded. "Did too."

Releasing Annabel's hand, Kaylee said, "Since you're all covered in mud, I think the odds were pretty fair, regardless of who started it. But you know what happens now, don't you?"

Jack eyed her with suspicion, looking far too much like his father, Tristan, right then and there. But Kaylee was used to all kinds of intimidating dragon-shifter looks by now and didn't miss a beat. "I'll have to hose you off in someone's backyard until you're clean."

"But it's cold!"

"It might snow!"

"That's mean!"

She shrugged, determined to tease them a little. "If you can stand throwing cold, wet mud, then you should be fine."

Annabel grunted—much like her father in that moment too—and said, "We can take our clothes off and shower inside."

Kaylee tapped her chin, as if thinking about it. "That might work, although it'd be more fun to use the outside hose."

Rhys sighed. "What if I clean up our dirty footprints after the shower? Will that work?"

Kaylee grinned. "That sounds like a plan. Now, let's head to Rhys's house, since it's the closest." Kayla quickly sent a text to Harris Chisholm and Dawn, letting them know she would be gone for a little while. Once she got a confirmation back, she herded the four children toward the house just down the pathway.

It was a sign of how cold and tired they were that the children barely argued on the way—the twins, in particular, always argued.

Soon enough, they all stood just inside the front door. Rhys's mom, Samira, appeared in the doorway and raised her brows. "Do I want to know?"

Kaylee laughed. "They need to wash off, and your place was the closest. Oh, and your son kindly offered to clean up any dirty footprints in the entryway after they're done."

Samira smiled and looked at the group of children. "Well, hurry up, then. I might just have some fresh biscuits for you, if there's time."

With that, the boys quickly stripped and dashed upstairs. Annabel lingered and sighed. "I don't want to share with them."

Samira gestured down the hall. "There's another shower down there, second door on the right."

Annabel undressed and streaked down the hallway. Once the door shut, Samira looked at Kaylee. "Come. You look like you could use a cup of tea."

When Kaylee had first arrived in the UK from the US, she'd hated tea. However, over time, it'd grown on her. It'd never replace coffee, but given how she was trying to limit caffeine because of her surprise pregnancy, it was the next best thing.

However, the second she reached the kitchen, a mixture of spices hit her nose and her stomach revolted. She barely made it to the sink before she threw up her breakfast.

By the time Kaylee finished, she was super embarrassed and a little lightheaded. After rinsing her mouth, she tried to stand up and toddled. Mentally, she cursed. She didn't know how much longer she could do this. Thanks to watching her sister's multiple pregnancies, Kaylee knew that shots of dragon's blood strengthened human women who carried and birthed a dragon-shifter's child. However, revealing that meant sharing her secret. And spilling that would not only make her sister Gina concerned, worried, and maybe even disappointed in her, but Kaylee's brothers-in-law would probably go on a manhunt of some sort to find the masked dragoman and do who the hell knew what with him.

The MacKenzies were a little crazy at times. Normally she loved them, but maybe not in this case.

Samira helped her to sit down and searched her gaze. After a beat, she asked softly, "Are you pregnant?"

Kaylee had done an amazing job of keeping herself together. But that one question broke down her walls and as soon as she said, "Yes," she started crying.

She was vaguely aware of Samira rubbing her back and then pulling her into a hug. She had only met the woman during the clan-wide dinner the night before, and yet she was being so nice to her.

Eventually, Kaylee got herself under control and stopped crying. Once she was mostly composed, Samira asked, "Does anyone else know?"

She bit her lip and shook her head. "I don't even know who the father is."

Samira studied her intensely. "Were you assaulted?"

She blinked. "No, no nothing like that. It was, well, a party where everyone wore masks. All I know is that he's a dragon-shifter."

She heard Samira suck in a breath, and she couldn't blame her. Having sex with a masked stranger wasn't exactly an everyday occurrence, especially when it was with a dragonman.

Samira's tone was kind but firm. "You need to go to the surgery straightaway."

Trying not to cry again, she met Samira's gaze again. "I can't."

"You can and you will. I don't want you to go through the same difficulties and worries I did when I carried Rhys. Things are so much better now for humans. You need to let Dr. Sid and the others help you, Kaylee, especially if you plan to keep the child."

Samira was also a human who had come to Stonefire years ago, before even Melanie Hall-MacLeod, and she had mated a dragonman named Liam. Back then, there had been less medical treatments for humans having dragon babies, and the risks had been high. Like, really high—as in nearly half of the pregnancies had ended up fatal for the mother.

Given that Kaylee hadn't had any treatments to date, and she was nearly three months along, she really should see a doctor.

And yet, if she did that, she'd have to tell not only her sister and in-laws, but Lochguard's clan leader as well. Disappointing Finn was the last thing she wanted to do, given how he'd worked so hard to allow her to stay with her sister despite not being mated to a dragon-shifter.

And yet, facing the music was better than ending up dead. Maybe. By just a little. Well, more than that since she did want to keep her baby. Part of the reason she'd gone to the party in the first place was because she'd been a little jealous of all the happy couples and families on Lochguard, and she'd thought that maybe she'd be lucky and find someone to mate. Because more than her sister, Kaylee had always wanted to be a wife and a mom.

She hadn't planned on it happening this way, though.

Placing a hand on her lower belly, she knew she needed to step up. The longer she put it off, the more she put both of them at risk.

Taking a deep breath, Kaylee finally met Samira's gaze again. "Okay, I'll go."

"Come, then. Let me just tell my mate I'll be back soon so he can keep an eye on the children." Samira went to the back door and let her mate know she was going out. And then they were soon bundled up and outside, walking toward Stonefire's little clinic.

The Brits called it a surgery, but that just sounded weird to Kaylee.

Once inside, Samira guided her to the front desk and was just about to ask the dragonman there about a visit when Kaylee heard a voice she knew well—that of Dr. Layla McFarland. "Kaylee. Are you all right, lass?"

She met Layla's eyes and did her best to look healthy. However, she must've failed because Layla murmured, "Come with me. You look far too pale for my liking."

Samira smiled at her and gave her hand a reassuring squeeze as she said, "It'll be fine, Kaylee, I believe that. If you ever need to talk to someone, find me anytime."

She nodded, thanked Samira, and then allowed Layla to take her to a small examination room. The dragon-shifter doctor gestured for Kaylee to sit down and then asked, "What's wrong?"

Shifting in her seat, she debated how to answer. Layla would have to tell Finn, and Kaylee didn't know what the Lochguard leader would do.

The doctor leaned in closer and then gasped. Layla moved back so she could see Kaylee's eyes again. "You're pregnant with a dragon-shifter's bairn?"

She muttered, "I thought only male dragons could smell it."

Layla lifted a dark brow. "I'm a doctor, remember? We're trained to pick up the scent when most female dragons wouldn't notice it. At least, not right away." She crossed her arms over her chest and asked, "Who's the father?"

She sighed. "I don't know." Then she straightened up, remembering she had someone else to fight for now. "But I'm keeping him or her, regardless."

Layla frowned. "You don't know who the father is?"

She bit her lip, but there was a knock at the door, followed by Dr. Gregor Innes's voice. "Can I come in?"

Layla replied, "Aye."

Once the tall, older doctor was in the room, he shut the door and looked her over with concern. Even though Gregor lived on Stonefire now, Kaylee had known him back when he lived on Lochguard. He'd delivered her sister's first baby, Jamie.

Gregor asked, "What's wrong, Kaylee?"

Layla didn't miss a beat. "She's pregnant and doesn't know the father. But I scented dragon-shifter, so there's that."

Kaylee's cheeks burned as Gregor approached her. "It's a long shot, but if you'll allow me, I might be able to pick up a scent. If I've ever met him, I should be able to place it."

She put her hands over her cheeks and closed her eyes, feeling beyond embarrassed. "Go for it."

Gregor came closer, and after a moment, he blurted, "When did you meet Maelon?"

Kaylee opened her eyes. "Who?"

"Dr. Maelon Perry, Snowridge's doctor. It's his scent mixed with yours. I know for sure it's him because he's here. Just like fingerprints, a dragon's scent is unique."

The blood drained from her face. "He's here?"

Gregor nodded. "Shall I fetch him?"

Kaylee's heart pounded in her chest as she tried to process Gregor's words. Yes, she'd dreamed of seeing the masked, dark-haired dragonman again. However, she hadn't expected him to be here, of all places. And his weird accent made sense now—he was Welsh.

Although was that better? Did it really matter?

She was more than aware she was putting off her answer, but her mind was a jumble. The whole point of the masquerade had been to keep their identities secret. Would Maelon be angry? Aloof? Dismiss her?

There was a small, very small, chance he might

want to get to know her. And yet, if he rejected her, it would sting.

Kaylee looked at each doctor in turn, trying to figure out how to answer. However, Layla's gentle voice garnered her attention. "You should probably tell him, Kaylee. I don't know what you two will do, but sooner or later, the DDA will ask about it. And they'll require you to reveal the father. Wouldn't it be better to let him hear it from you first?"

She glanced down at her hands. Her sister had always cautioned that her rash behavior and reckless decisions would catch up with her. Kaylee had tried her best to be better in Scotland, but one slip up had undone all that. Gina would be beyond disappointed in her, and that would probably be the worst thing of all since her sister's opinion mattered more to her than anyone else in the world.

Layla touched her arm, and Kaylee met her flashing dragon eyes. The doctor said softly, "Maelon's a nice enough bloke, and handsome as well. He wouldn't hurt you, lass. If that's what you're afraid of."

Kaylee shook her head. "I never felt threatened by him. That's not it."

True enough, she'd felt comfortable which is why she'd ended up having a one-night stand with the guy. As a rule, she didn't do that.

Now she understood why she shouldn't have.

Layla asked, "Then what is it?"

She blurted, "Will I be forced to mate him?"

"I honestly don't know, Kaylee. It's possible Finn can work out a deal with the DDA for you to live on Lochguard with your bairn. Unless…"

Her voice trailed off and Kaylee asked, "Unless what?"

"Unless Maelon wants to claim his child. Then I'm not sure what will happen. Nearly always the dragon-shifter parent is given precedence over the human one. Which means you'll have to mate him to stay with the wee one."

The thought of having to mate a dragon-shifter just to have a claim on her child, like in the days of old when men always had the rights over women, made her angry.

It's just a taste of how the dragon-shifter world is different from the human one, Kaylee. You'd better get used to it since you'll have a little dragon baby soon enough.

She took a deep breath, trying to tame her anger. After all, she might be getting ahead of herself. The dragonman might not even want a child. If that was the case, she could live on Lochguard near her sister and their children could grow up together.

Except she didn't know what this Dr. Maelon Perry would want. There was no way around it—she'd have to talk to him.

Before she could change her mind, she said, "I need to see him."

There was no confusion about the him in question. Layla nodded and glanced at Gregor. The dragonman nodded. "Aye, I'll fetch him. But are you sure you want to do this now? You might want to rest first. I'm not sure how Maelon will react to the news."

Kaylee shook her head. "No, I want to do it now. If I wait, I'll just keep thinking about what-ifs, and it'll drive me crazy."

Layla added, "Besides, Kaylee needs to get a shot of dragon's blood as soon as possible. The father's works best, aye?"

Kaylee jumped in, "But Gina didn't have the father's blood for her first pregnancy. And she was fine."

Layla replied, "Aye, but I think that's because Fergus was her true mate, and so his blood helped her." She paused and then asked, "Did Maelon kiss you?"

She mumbled, "No."

That had been one of the rules of the masquerade —no kissing on the lips. Which made sense since a kiss could set off a mate-claim frenzy for a dragon-shifter and that would've disturbed the secret party.

Gregor went to the door. "Aye, well, let's talk to Maelon and go from there."

Once the door shut, Kaylee asked Layla, "Do you like him?"

"Maelon? Aye, well enough. He's come a long way, that's for sure. He doubted Sid's abilities at first, but I think having his clan leader mated to someone like Delaney has changed his mind about females quite a bit." She opened her mouth to ask more questions, but Layla shook her head and beat her to it. "I think it's best if you talk with him to make judgments for yourself, aye?"

With a sigh, Kaylee muttered her agreement. And as she waited, she shifted in her seat, wondering about the dragonman who had changed her life forever.

Chapter Thirteen

Dr. Maelon Perry was going over some of Trahern's notes when there was a knock on the door. Trahern frowned, but didn't bother to check who was there.

To some, the male's behavior would be strange but Maelon had known Trahern nearly his whole life. Before moving to Stonefire, Trahern had lived on Snowridge in Wales, where they'd both grown up.

While odd at times, Trahern was clever and one of the few minds who kept up with Maelon's own. He didn't realize how much he'd missed the other dragonman until he'd been gone.

The knocking increased in volume, and Maelon went to answer it; on the other side of it stood Gregor. Even if they hadn't known each other long—only since Gregor's mate had managed to get them all to work together for medical research—the male was nice enough and competent. However, his eyes were flashing rapidly, full of a mixture of emotions Maelon couldn't make out. "Yes?"

Gregor said, "I need you to come with me."

His tone was a bit sterner than normal. "Why?"

"Just come with me, aye? There's something I need to discuss with you."

He was about to say he was busy when Maelon's dragon spoke up. *Something is wrong. Don't argue for once.*

I don't argue for the sake of it.

Yes, you do. Don't ruin the new friendships with the other doctors.

His dragon had somehow ended up being one of the few in the world who cared about human-type rules and niceties. Probably out of necessity, since Maelon tended to be blunter and more honest than anyone liked.

He replied to his beast, *I don't understand you sometimes.*

His dragon huffed. *Good. Dragons should be mysterious.*

He nearly chuckled, but instead focused on Gregor. "Okay, but not for long. I'm helping Trahern with one of his formulas."

Gregor nodded and turned. "Let's just go down the hall, aye?"

The Scottish dragonman's usual humor was absent. Had something gone wrong? Had some of Maelon's suggestions for helping Jane Hartley made her condition worse?

No, that couldn't be it. He never gave suggestions unless they were sound, meaning the reward was greater than the risk.

They stopped in front of one of the smaller

examination rooms. Gregor glanced at him and said, "Prepare yourself, lad."

He frowned at the cryptic remark, but then the Scot opened the door and walked inside. Maelon followed, but quickly stopped in his tracks as he noticed the female sitting in the room.

Not just any female, but *her*. The one with slightly wild, curly brown hair, pale skin dotted with freckles, and brown eyes that bordered on golden.

Much like that night he'd seen her across the room at the masquerade, her beauty stunned him a second. But then his rational side took charge again, and he asked, "What the bloody hell is going on here?"

The female flinched, and his dragon growled. *Stop being an arsehole and be nicer.*

His dragon was usually right about these things, so Maelon cleared his throat and said, "Apologies. I'm surprised, is all, and a bit confused."

Even with his awkward social skills, he knew that blurting out they'd shagged at a masquerade three months ago probably wasn't the best idea.

Then he really looked at the female—they'd never exchanged names—and noticed her eyes were slightly puffy, she had circles under her eyes, and she was far too pale. Something was wrong.

His doctor's instinct to help kicked in, and he walked over to her. He stopped right in front of her and was about to ask what was wrong when he was hit with a scent he'd hoped never to smell—his scent intertwined with a female's.

She was pregnant. With his child.

He took a few steps backward, trying to make sense of the situation.

Gregor's voice filled the room. "Aye, now you know. The question is—what do you plan to do about it?"

What was he going to do? He had no fucking idea, that was for sure.

His dragon growled. *You may never have wanted a child, but the deed is done. Will you abandon him or her? Really?*

You're just saying that because you've always wanted children.

No, I'm thinking of the human female. Look at her, really look at her. She's having a hard time carrying our child. If we don't help, she could die.

Maelon had never really had to worry about a human carrying a dragon-shifter's child before. Mostly because Snowridge hadn't had any human mates until their clan leader, Rhydian, had mated the human female named Delaney. By then, they'd had the means and knowledge to make her pregnancy easier. More than one, actually, as the pair seemed intent on repopulating Snowridge on their own.

But it was true—before Sid's research and trials, human females hadn't had high survival rates. And if this human female looked this bad this early, she needed treatment.

Specifically, shots of his dragon's blood would work best.

Maelon may never have wanted to be a father, but he had a deep-seated need to save lives. He couldn't willingly let her suffer. Which meant his life was about to change forever.

He cleared his throat. "I'll shift and need someone

to draw some blood. She'll need it right away." He turned toward the door, but the female's American accent reached his ears. "Wait a second."

Frowning, he turned his head over his shoulder. "Yes?"

She bit her bottom lip, but Maelon forced himself not to think of the last time she'd done it, as he'd stroked between her thighs.

She said, "Don't you even want to know my name?"

"I suppose."

Fire flickered in her gaze. "Never mind. Just go away."

Impatience raced through him. "Excuse me for wanting to heal you. By all means, let's chat a bit."

Gregor growled, "Maelon."

"What? Every second we waste on niceties, the greater the chance her health will turn for the worst. I'll help her first and talk later. I'll be behind the surgery, so send someone to draw the blood."

As he walked down the hall and toward the back door, his dragon grunted. *You were rude to her.*

I don't care. I'd rather be brusque than watch her suffer.

What do you plan to do about her and the baby?

Maelon didn't answer. His father had been murdered by dragon hunters, and his mother had been so grief-stricken that she'd committed suicide soon after. In the end, her love for her mate had been greater than that for her son.

Soon after, he'd vowed never to take a mate or have children. That way, he'd never have to worry about disappointing or abandoning them.

Now, he didn't know what the fuck he was going to do.

Regardless, he would focus on the most pressing issues for the moment. Once he shucked his clothes, he focused on wings sprouting from his back, his nose elongating into a snout, and his arms and legs growing into limbs. When he stood in his gold dragon form, he stretched his wings and itched to jump into the air, return to Snowridge, and back to his ordered life.

Except as Gregor came out with the necessary supplies to draw some dragon's blood, Maelon knew he couldn't do that.

Bloody hell, he'd have to talk to Rhydian about this.

His dragon asked, *And what about the female?*

I need to think on it.

Stop being an arsehole.

Maelon ignored his beast and waited for Gregor to finish. However, the dragonman kept the needle in place, even after completing the blood draw, knowing full well Maelon couldn't move until he removed it.

Gregor eyed him as he said, "Her name is Kaylee MacDonald. And if you hurt her, you'll be dealing with not only Lochguard, but Stonefire. So tread carefully, aye?"

Gregor's usual friendliness was gone, replaced with a steely gaze.

Fuck. The complications to his life had already begun.

Not wanting to burn bridges, Maelon nodded. Satisfied, Gregor left and allowed Maelon to shift back into his human form. Once he was dressed, he went looking for his clan leader.

His dragon sighed. *And the female?*

Later. I need to make sure Snowridge will be a safe place for her before I make any kind of decision.

Maybe she doesn't want to come to Snowridge. If you talked to her, you could find out.

I won't propose anything I can't follow through on. Now, hush. I see Rhydian just up ahead.

The Welsh leader was, in fact, with his human mate. Delaney noticed him first and started to raise a hand in greeting when her brows came together. As soon as he stopped in front of him, Delaney asked, "What the bloody hell is wrong?"

At first, Maelon hadn't known what to expect of the human. But over time, he'd come to appreciate her manner. She'd also learned to trust him, after helping with her pregnancies.

He cleared his throat. "Can I chat with you both for a second?"

Rhydian's brows shot up at that. "You better start talking."

Maelon told them the main points about meeting the human at a party, sleeping with her, and just now finding out she was pregnant. At the end of it, Delaney asked, "She isn't your true mate, then?"

He shook his head. "I don't know. Between the alcohol dulling my senses and no kissing on the mouth, I couldn't tell."

Rhydian stared at him. Hard. "And this is why dragon-shifters shouldn't drink, aye? Now she's pregnant, and you won't be able to tell unless you kiss her because your dragon will be drawn to the child over any true mate pull. But putting that aside for a moment, what does she want to do?"

"I don't know. I didn't ask her."

Delaney narrowed her eyes. "You didn't ask her? Are you serious?"

His dragon sat, smugly, but didn't say anything. His posture alone said, "I told you so."

Ignoring his beast, he replied, "My first concern was for her health. Besides, I didn't know what to say or do. She should probably live with Snowridge until the baby is born, at least, so I can give her my dragon's blood. But is the clan safe for her?"

Even though Delaney was human and lived on Snowridge, she was a former professional boxer who could take care of herself. The human female—Kaylee, he reminded himself—was far more delicate. She was kind, funny, and full of life. That was what had drawn him in the first place.

However, she was also young, probably naïve, and wouldn't be able to knock out someone who tried to hurt her, like Delaney could do. And even if he didn't know Kaylee, he wouldn't risk her life unnecessarily.

Rhydian crossed his arms over his chest. "It should be by now. The rogue Protectors were handed over to the Department of Dragon Affairs, and I've slowly 'retired' the most vocal of the older clan members to the outlying homes, bordering the farms."

Unlike most clans, Snowridge was situated mostly inside a set of mountains. They had a series of outlying farms to help feed the clan, though. And Rhydian had built small cottages in the most unproductive areas to give those who mistrusted humans a place to live without being banished—it was easier to monitor them that way.

Maelon nodded. "Then she should move to Snowridge until the child is born. I'll make sure she survives it."

Delaney asked drolly, "Have you considered the fact she might not want to move to Snowridge and be away from her family? She's only on Lochguard because of her sister, that much I do know. Which probably means she's close to her."

Maelon shrugged. "It's not forever. And I would think she would want her best chance at survival."

Delaney rolled her eyes. "You're brilliant when it comes to medicine, but sometimes you're a bloody eejit, Maelon." She glanced at her mate. "You can deal with him. I'm going to talk to this Kaylee and see what she wants to do."

Maelon was about to protest, but Rhydian said, "Let her go, Maelon. You and I need to talk to Finn. Even if she doesn't want to move to Snowridge, he needs to know about this. Especially if the human does want to stay with us for a bit."

He knew better than to argue with his clan leader, and so they headed toward the cottage where Finn and his mate were staying.

Then he remembered Finn's mate was close to birthing their fourth child. Bloody fantastic. That meant Finn would be less congenial than normal, no doubt.

His dragon spoke up. *Maybe try to be nice and follow social niceties for once.*

Maelon merely grunted in reply.

Rhydian knocked, and Finn opened it shortly thereafter. As the Scottish clan leader glanced between him and Rhydian, he asked, "What's happened?"

Gesturing toward Maelon, Rhydian answered, "He's the father of Kaylee MacDonald's child."

Finn's eyes widened, his pupils flashing rapidly. "What?"

Rhydian frowned. "You didn't know?"

Finn eyed Maelon closely, his tone steely as he asked, "Did you take advantage of her?"

"No," he replied.

Finn looked unconvinced—maybe there was a story there that he didn't know—and stepped back. "You two had better come inside. We'll chat before I send for Kaylee."

Soon, they all sat and discussed the events. Eventually, Kaylee arrived with Delaney. Since her coloring was better, she must've received her first shot of dragon's blood.

The human female never once looked at him, though. No, she merely sat, looked at Finn, and waited, as if expecting a scolding.

However, Finn merely softened his expression and said, "No worries, lass. I'll help you any way you need."

Maelon nearly said he'd help her, but bit his tongue. He said to his dragon, *Stop it.*

I didn't do anything.

You did. You want to protect her.

Yes, I do. But maybe you do too.

With a mental grunt, he didn't say anything else while he waited to see what came next.

Chapter Fourteen

Kaylee's jaw had dropped when Dr. Maelon Perry had left the examination room, not even caring about what her name was.

Gone was the intense, sexy dragonman from a few months ago. In his place was a man too highhanded and cocky for his own good.

Layla tried to calm her down. But Kaylee's mind raced, barely registering anything until Dr. Innes returned with a vial of dark red dragon's blood. Within seconds of it being injected, her dizziness faded, and she felt a little stronger. Time would tell if it helped with her nausea or not.

Soon there was a knock, and the dark-haired form of Delaney Griffiths, the mate of Snowridge's leader, walked in. Delaney shook her head as she said, "Sorry about Maelon. His manners are shite, but he's a brilliant doctor." The woman stared at her a second before asking, "How are you?"

Kaylee's eyes heated, but she forced herself not to

cry. She'd held it together this long, and she could do it a little longer.

Something must've shown on her face, however, because Delaney placed a hand over hers and squeezed. "Rhydian won't make you do anything you don't want to do. And even if you're not mated to a dragon-shifter, you've lived with them long enough to know they can be high-handed at times and you've probably learned how to stand up to them."

Kaylee bobbed her head. "Yes. But he's just so… different from before."

Delaney tilted her head. "Maelon tends to keep to himself, so if he showed a bit of himself, he must've felt comfortable around you, aye?"

"Maybe," she mumbled. The alcohol involved had probably been a bigger influence, though. But she didn't mention it.

Delaney's cell phone beeped, and she checked it. "Come on, Kaylee. Rhydian and Maelon are with Finn. It's best to get this over with now. I'm sure keeping it a secret has taken its toll, aye?"

She gave a wobbly smile. "I guess."

Kaylee waved goodbye to Layla and was grateful that Delaney didn't try to make small talk. The woman was a lot older than Kaylee, and taller, too. She definitely looked like the type of person who could stand up to a dragon-shifter better than she could. After all, Kaylee was short, not really that much in shape, and definitely lacking in the muscle department.

They arrived at Finn's cottage, and a very pregnant Arabella opened the door. She smiled at Kaylee and said, "Finn has your back, Kaylee. Don't worry."

She nodded, her throat growing tight with emotion. "I know I should've said something."

Arabella pulled her in for a hug—well as best she could, given how pregnant she was. "Don't worry about it." She pulled back. "Besides, Finn owes you for how much you've helped me. You're brilliant with the triplets."

Kaylee had grown closer with Arabella over the last six months or so, once she'd helped out the dragonwoman regularly with watching her children. It was a far cry from the first time she'd met Arabella, when the dragonwoman had seemed distant and a little intimidating because of the scars on her face and healed burns on her neck.

But Arabella was kind at heart and loved Lochguard nearly as much as her own family. Not to mention she helped keep Finn balanced and sane, which many people probably didn't realize.

Just the thought of not seeing the triplets several times a week brought back the stupid stinging to her eyes. But considering nothing had been decided, Kaylee swallowed and composed herself. "I'm ready to see Finn."

Arabella gestured down the hall. "You'd best go in. I'll stay in the kitchen, otherwise Finn will be distracted. I'm always here if you need to talk."

"Thanks, Ara."

After smiling at the dragonwoman, Kaylee took a deep breath and went to the door indicated and knocked. Finn answered, his eyes kind. Regardless, she felt awful for hiding anything from him.

From the corner of her eye, she noticed Maelon

and Rhydian. Deliberately not looking at the doctor, she focused on Finn. He said softly, "No worries, lass. I'll help you any way you need."

A tear did escape then, and Kaylee brushed it away. "I'm sorry."

Finn handed her a tissue, and she took it. He said, "No more apologies, lass. Now, we need to discuss your future. You have two choices at this point—stay on Lochguard and we'll find dragon's blood donors to help you. Layla will probably have the best recommendation as to who, or Dr. Sid will. The other option is to go to Snowridge for the duration of your pregnancy and Maelon will provide you with dragon's blood. The latter is slightly better for you and the bairn, but only by a little."

Still not looking at Maelon, Kaylee asked, "Will I be able to keep the baby? Or will *he* try to take it?"

Maelon spoke up. "I have no desire to raise children. I will provide assistance, if you need it. But I won't try to get custody."

Kaylee finally looked at Maelon. His face was unreadable, although his pupils flashed rapidly. Before she could think better of it, she blurted, "What's your dragon saying?"

It was bad manners to ask, but she didn't care. Given how he'd been an asshole earlier, he couldn't expect her to be all kind and polite, as if nothing had happened.

Her sister might say she should try. But when Kaylee's temper started to show, it usually didn't bode well for anyone.

And given how Maelon glanced away from her, it definitely stoked her temper.

He looked at the wall as he replied, "That's private."

Rhydian growled. "Bloody hell, Maelon. What's wrong with you? I know you don't care for social niceties, but this female carries your child. You could try a little harder."

Finn's steely voice made Kaylee blink since her clan leader rarely lost his good humor. "I'm not sure I want Kaylee to go anywhere if this is how you're going to treat her."

The tension in the room was thick, and having lived with dragon-shifters for a while now, Kaylee knew that if she didn't do something, things would go south. Fast.

She stood, grateful that she was steady on her feet, and stated, "I have a question for you, Dr. Perry."

His eyes finally met hers, his gaze intent, and it reminded her of when they'd first met.

Not wanting to go down that road—yes, sex with him had been great but didn't matter any longer—she continued, "Why me? Of all the people there, why did you pick me?"

For a second, she thought he wouldn't answer. Then he said quietly, "You're so full of life. I couldn't resist it."

His answer made her pause. Normally, when not struggling with nausea and carrying a dragon's baby, she was more carefree and playful. She was the one asking to slide down a dragon's side like a slide or picking flowers to make into a crown or even laying in the grass to stare up at the stars and make up her own constellations, complete with stories.

Not backing down now, she asked, "Why couldn't you resist?"

Maelon still stared at her, his pupils flashing to slits and back, before he said, "My childhood ended early, and I had to grow up quickly. That night, you made me feel as if I could let go and have fun, uncaring about any responsibilities for once. That's why."

For a few beats, there was no one else in the room but the two of them. She wanted to ask him what had happened, why he didn't let go sometimes, or why he'd turned into the icicle of a man compared to before.

But then Maelon cleared his throat and looked away again, quickly as if burned.

Maybe it was stupid and she'd come to regret it. However, she wanted the chance to get to know him better. For the sake of her baby, of course. That's what mattered.

Okay, and maybe a teeny, tiny bit for herself.

"I want to go to Snowridge until the baby is born, provided you agree to two conditions."

Rhydian asked, "Which are?"

"Dr. Perry is required to have two meals with me each week, at a place of my choosing."

Rhydian frowned. "As long as it's cleared with my Protectors, that should be fine. What's the other?"

"I want to work with the children on Snowridge while I'm there. I need to keep busy, or I'll go crazy."

Rhydian frowned, but Delaney—who currently sat in his lap—answered before her mate, "I think that's brilliant. The more humans the kids are exposed to, the better."

Since the doctor hadn't said anything, she tested out his first name. "Maelon? Do you agree?"

He glanced at her and then away. "Yes."

Kaylee had been upset before at Maelon looking away. But she'd noticed something—he didn't really look anyone in the eye, and if so, then not for long. Was there a reason for it?

Crap, now she really did want to talk to him more and find out the answers. Her curiosity was going to get the better of her someday, that was for sure.

She looked at Rhydian and then Finn. "Is that okay?"

Finn nodded. "I'll add regular check-ins to the requirements, and some visits from Lochguard clan members, just to check in on your health."

Rhydian grunted. "Aye, that's fine with me. When?"

Kaylee bit her bottom lip and then answered, "Not long after the gathering. I need to pack and convince my sister and her mate not to follow me to Wales."

Finn chuckled. "Good luck with that. Gina is protective of you, which means so is Fergus. But don't worry—I'll help where I can. Even if it means I'm losing the best part-time nanny in the world for my triplets."

Kaylee smiled at Finn. "There are a few people I know of who could help you."

"You and I will chat some more later, Kaylee. For now, we all need to rest tonight and get ready for the celebration tomorrow." He stood. "Unless you need me to leave you alone with your mate, Rhydian. You seem quite cozy in that chair together, aye?"

Rhydian glared, but Delaney laughed. "Maybe

some other time. We need to check on our children and feed those wee rascals, too."

She stood, along with Rhydian. They both nodded at her, mentioning they'd talk soon, and left. Finn looked between her and Maelon and moved to the door. "I can leave you two alone a bit, aye?"

The burst of energy she'd received from the dragon's blood was fading. She simply didn't have the energy to deal with the dragon doctor right now. So she shook her head. "I'll talk to him on Snowridge. I need some time to prepare."

With that, she left, unaware of Maelon's gaze following her every movement as she left.

Chapter Fifteen

The next evening, Kai tried not to hover. However, he kept remembering when Jane had fainted two days ago and then he needed to be near his mate to soothe man and beast.

Except as he tried to follow Jane into the bathroom, she stopped and placed a hand on his chest. "I think I can sit on the toilet by myself, Kai."

"It's the getting up again that I'm worried about."

She sighed and stroked his chest. Her touch helped to ease him a little. "The extra treatments are already helping. And Dr. Sid said I could go for an hour or so tonight without worry, as long as I use a wheelchair. And since this evening is historic, with so many dragon clans together to celebrate the Winter Solstice, I don't want to miss it." She stood on her tiptoes to kiss him before murmuring, "I'll tell you if I get too tired and need to leave."

His dragon grunted. *I trust our mate. You should too.*

Of course I trust her. But I'm just worried.

Jane just wants our support. Give it to her.

He cupped his mate's cheek. "Okay. But if you so much as sway or stumble, I'm taking you home, no questions asked."

She smiled at him. "Unless we're dancing, and then the stumbling will be because you have two left feet."

He frowned. "You're not going to dance."

Jane nipped his bottom lip. "Probably not. But just don't expect me to sit in a corner with you in front of me, scowling to keep everyone away. I won't be caged like that, Kai. And more importantly—I won't let you."

He sighed. "I know, Janey. I'm trying my best, but it's hard." He stroked her cheek. "I can't lose you."

She smiled at him. "And you won't, you bloody dragonman. I'm too stubborn to go easily." Her face softened. "I love you, Kai."

"I love you too, Janey."

"Good. So maybe now you won't be offended when I say if you come into this bathroom before I'm ready to come out, I will punch you in the bollocks."

His lips twitched. "You would too."

She winked and then went into the bathroom. Kai quickly changed into his traditional dragon-shifter outfit. It was like a type of kilt, with fabric gathered around the waist and a sash thrown across his chest and over his shoulder. The cold didn't bother him, so he didn't don the crisp white shirt that some would wear during the winter months.

He'd just finished getting ready when Jane exited the bathroom, and he took in her attire. She had on the female version of the traditional dress, which was loose and pinned across one shoulder. Her arms were covered with a shawl of iridescent black, which made the deep red of her dress stand out even more.

He growled, "Even if I know I can't, I still want to rip that dress from your body and fuck you against the wall. Now."

She raised a dark eyebrow. "The last time you did that you promised not to destroy any more of my traditional dresses. They're bloody expensive, and it's a bit embarrassing asking for another one."

Kai itched to undo the pin at her shoulder anyway, but his dragon spoke up. *Remember what the doctor said.*

Fuck. It's going to be a long few weeks.

Dr. Sid had said no sex for at least three weeks, as a precaution. Until Jane's levels were all normal again, the doctor didn't want to take any risks.

His dragon grunted. *Maybe. But Jane wants the baby, and we'd do anything to ensure her wish comes true.*

Jane walked up to him and took one of his hands in hers. "Time will go fast enough. Besides, once the doctor gives the okay, I might even fulfill one of your fantasies to thank you."

He shook his head. "I don't need a reward to wait, Janey. Just having you in my arms will be enough."

"Kai."

He kissed her gently and then pulled away. "Now, let's go and celebrate with everyone else."

"Nearly everyone else. I feel bad that Nikki and Rafe won't be able to attend."

"They have an early Winter Solstice present of their own. I'm sure I'll have to look at like five hundred bloody photos tomorrow, anyway."

Jane laughed. "Be nice. Because I'm sure you'll be the exact same way when we have a child."

She moved toward the door, but he pulled her back to him. "No matter what happens, I think we should take in one of the orphans."

"Are you sure?"

He nodded. "That way I can train the older sibling to protect the younger one."

She grinned at him. "You would think that way." Her expression softened. "But it'd be nice. Despite how much Rafe can be a pain, I love my brother and couldn't imagine life without him." She placed a hand over her lower belly. "I'd like this little one to have that same sort of relationship."

Kai placed his hand over hers. "Then I'll make sure to be the first to apply, once the applications are open."

She tilted her head up, and he kissed her. Slowly, taking his time to explore her mouth, before he pulled away and Jane said, "I can't wait until you have more than one person to give you dragon cuddles. It's going to be a daily thing."

He grunted, and she laughed.

But Kai pulled his mate against his body, kissed her hair, and reveled in her heat and scent. "Only for you, Janey. Only for you."

Once Jane sat in the wheelchair, the pair left and went to join in the mixture of Christmas and Winter Solstice with the other dragon clan leaders, clan members, and everyone on Stonefire.

The great hall was decorated in a mixture of winter decorations—such as snowflakes, icicles, and some winter plants—and some human Christmas ones, including a large Christmas tree in one corner.

Strange to think that less than a decade ago, the event would've been only those of Stonefire, and almost no human attendees. Now humans were everywhere, not to mention all the visitors from the other dragon clans. Things had changed so much in such a short time.

As if sensing Kai's thoughts, Jane raised a hand to touch one of his arms just behind her, on the handlebars of the wheelchair, garnering his attention. She said, "Did you ever think things would end up like this?"

He leaned down and kissed her cheek. "No. But whilst the changes in our clans and the others are important, the best thing I ever did was agree to work with a stubborn reporter who didn't think much of putting herself in danger."

She gave a half-hearted glare. "I knew what I was doing." He raised his brows and she huffed. "Mostly."

He kissed her cheek again and whispered, "You're brilliant, Janey. But we're better together."

She smiled up at him. "Yes, we are."

As they stared at one another, the love in Jane's eyes making his heart swell, Kai moved to kiss her, uncaring who saw.

Because Jane Hartley was his love, his mate, his everything. And he couldn't wait until they started the next chapter of their lives as parents, one way or another.

He murmured, "I love you," before someone called out his name and he wheeled his mate over to where

Aaron and Teagan stood with Bram and Evie. And as they all chatted about the celebration and what to expect in the new year, Kai held Jane's hand and felt a measure of peace and happiness he never would've expected all those years ago, when his true mate had rejected him.

But in fact, that had been his good fortune. Because Kai was right where he belonged, with the mate he wanted, and he could face anything with Jane by his side.

Epilogue

Just Over Eight Months Later

J ane leaned against Kai's side, staring down at the little bundle in her arms, and tried her best not to cry. After a grueling eight months—full of medications and injections and multiple doctor visits— Jane had become the first known case of a human incompatible with dragon-shifters to birth a dragon-shifter's child.

Her son was a miracle, plain and simple. And she still had trouble believing he was real.

Kai kissed her cheek and adjusted the blanket around their son, Matthew. "He's perfect."

Matthew had light blond hair, the same color Kai had possessed as a child. He was wrinkly like all newborns, but Jane didn't care. She touched his nose. "I think he looks like you."

"Maybe. But I hope he ends up looking like both of us."

They stared a little longer, both memorizing the moment with their new baby, when someone knocked. Her brother poked his head inside. "Are you all right, Janey?"

She smiled. "Tired, but well enough. Come in."

Rafe entered. Right behind him was Jane and Kai's adopted son, Caleb. He was tall for a six-year-old, and had huge brown eyes that took everything in.

Kai was convinced Caleb would be a Protector one day.

Jane motioned for him to come closer. "Come meet your baby brother."

The little boy approached slowly until he was at Jane's side. He said, "He's wrinkly."

Jane laughed. "Yes, he is. But Matthew will fill out soon enough, I'm sure." She reached out a hand and brushed some black hair from Caleb's forehead. "You have a very important job now, don't you?"

Caleb nodded. "Dad said I have to watch over him. It's my first assignment."

Kai grunted. "That's right. And a very important one too."

Rafe ruffled Caleb's hair. "Maybe once you get some practice, you can look after your cousins, too."

Caleb smiled, which made Jane do the same. The boy had been unsure at first since he'd never had a family. However, since Jane had mostly been on bedrest for her pregnancy, she'd spent a lot of her time reading to Caleb, talking with him, learning more about him. He was definitely more comfortable with Jane than

Kai. However, the little boy did everything he could to impress his new dad. It was sweet, really, to see Kai and Caleb together. Kai didn't show his softer side to many, but it'd touched Jane that her gruff dragonman had done so with their oldest son.

Jane patted the spot beside her on the bed. "Come sit with us."

Rafe helped Caleb up, and the little boy leaned against Jane's side, much like he'd done over the last few months when he was tired.

There was another knock, and Bram entered the room. He grinned as he walked toward the bed. "I heard it's another boy. In twenty or so years, are we going to have two more Protectors?"

Jane rolled her eyes. "Don't encourage Kai. This one isn't even a day old yet."

Bram winked, walked closer and said, "I'll wait until he at least starts walking." He smiled at them both. "Congratulations."

Jane shared a glance with Kai. "Thank you."

Caleb asked, "Is he going to sleep all the time? The babies in the orphanage slept all the time. It was boring."

Jane laughed. "In the beginning, we all sleep a lot. It just gives him time to get used to us and for us to get used to him." She put an arm around Caleb. "Just like when he was in my belly, I'll still need your help. So I doubt you'll be bored."

Caleb gave a shy smile. "I'll help you, Mum. I always will."

Jane sucked in a breath—this was the first time Caleb had called her Mum. Tears pricked her eyes, but she did her best to keep them at bay. Even though they were happy tears, she didn't want to upset Caleb. "Of course you will. You're a brilliant little boy, love."

As Caleb talked to his new brother, Jane shared a look with Kai and smiled. He mouthed, "I love you," and she did the same.

Before she knew it, her parents and Nikki and her girls were there, cooing over the baby and all sharing how they intended to spoil him.

Eventually, Kai noticed how tired Jane was and ushered them all out, except for Caleb. He'd fallen asleep at Jane's side, and she didn't have the heart to wake him up.

Kai leaned against the bed, so that Caleb was between them, and then wrapped his arms around Jane, Caleb, and Matthew. He kissed Jane's forehead. "Everything I ever wanted is in my arms right now."

Maybe some would think it was flattery, but Jane saw the truth in her eyes. Over the course of her pregnancy, her lingering doubts about not being Kai's true mate had fled. Kai belonged to her as much as she belonged to him. Together, they were unstoppable. "Kiss me, Kai."

He gently pressed his lips to hers, and she sighed as Kai said, "Now, let me give you lots of dragon cuddles before you need to rest."

She smiled and leaned against her boys, happy and grateful and full of love. She had her happy ending now, and she couldn't wait to see what her future held.

I hoped you enjoyed this follow-up story and the final happy ending for Kai and Jane. :) If you guessed Kaylee and Maelon's story is next, you're right! After a one-night stand with a Welsh dragoman leaves Kaylee pregnant, she goes to stay on Snowridge until the baby is born. He's determined to never be a father, but she sees past his walls to the hurting dragonman underneath…

The **MASKED DRAGON OF SNOWRIDGE** will be available in print in early 2024.

Author's Note

Well, here we are at the end of another mega-follow-up story! I hope you enjoyed the little updates from the various couples. I'm unsure if I'll do another one of these (maybe toward the very, very end of the series), mainly because it takes me the same amount of time to research and write this novella as it does to write a full-length new book!

This book also helps set up addressing one of the loose ends I have in the series—Kaylee MacDonald. I figured out a few books ago that she wouldn't find her happy ending on Lochguard, and so it had to be with another clan. And, well, I figured Snowridge is finally ready to welcome another human female. Poor Delaney could use some company, don't you think? Maelon Perry has showed up a few times before, but never in a major way. He's an interesting one, though. You'll just have to wait and see what happens with this grumpy/sunshine pair!

As always, I want to thank my beta readers—

Sabrina D., Iliana G., Ashley B., and Mel M. They are amazing women who volunteer their time to read, comment, and find the minor inconsistencies and/or typos for me. I truly value and appreciate their hard work.

And lastly, a huge thank to you, the reader, for your support. Without you, I wouldn't be able to write these wonderful stories and revisit characters that have become like family to me. Thank you and I'll see you at the end of the next book!

Also by Jessie Donovan

Dark Lords of London

Vampire's Modern Bride (DLL #1)

Vampire's Fae Witch Healer (DLL #2)

Fae Witch's Vampire Guard (DLL #3)

Vampires' Shared Bride (DLL #4 / TBD)

Dragon Clan Gatherings

Summer at Lochguard (DCG #1)

Winter at Stonefire (DCG #2)

Kelderan Runic Warriors

The Conquest (KRW #1)

The Barren (KRW #2)

The Heir (KRW #3)

The Forbidden (KRW #4)

The Hidden (KRW #5)

The Survivor (KRW #6)

Lochguard Highland Dragons

The Dragon's Dilemma (LHD #1)

The Dragon Guardian (LHD #2)

The Dragon's Heart (LHD #3)

The Dragon Warrior (LHD #4)

The Dragon Family (LHD #5)

The Dragon's Discovery (LHD #6)

The Dragon's Pursuit (LHD #7)

The Dragon Collective (LHD #8)

The Dragon's Chance (LHD # 9)

The Dragon's Memory (LHD #10)

The Dragon Recruit / Iris & Antony (LHD #11, TBD)

Stonefire Dragons

Sacrificed to the Dragon (SD #1)

Seducing the Dragon (SD #2)

Revealing the Dragons (SD #3)

Healed by the Dragon (SD #4)

Reawakening the Dragon (SD #5)

Loved by the Dragon (SD #6)

Surrendering to the Dragon (SD #7)

Cured by the Dragon (SD #8)

Aiding the Dragon (SD #9)

Finding the Dragon (SD #10)

Craved by the Dragon (SD #11)

Persuading the Dragon (SD #12)

Treasured by the Dragon (SD #13)

Trusting the Dragon (SD #14)

Taught by the Dragon (SD #15)

Charming the Dragon / Hayley & Nathan (SD #16 / 2024)

Stonefire Dragons Shorts

Meeting the Humans (SDS #1)

The Dragon Camp (SDS #2)

The Dragon Play (SDS #3)

Dragon's First Christmas (SDS #4)

Stonefire Dragons Universe

Winning Skyhunter (SDU #1)

Transforming Snowridge (SDU #2)

Finding Dragon's Court (SDU #3)

Masked Dragon of Snowridge (SDU #4 / January 2024)

Tahoe Dragon Mates

The Dragon's Choice (TDM #1)

The Dragon's Need (TDM #2)

The Dragon's Bidder (TDM #3)

The Dragon's Charge (TDM #4)

The Dragon's Weakness (TDM #5)

The Dragon's Find (TDM #6)

The Dragon's Surprise / Dr. Kyle Baker & Alexis (TDM #7 / TBD)

Asylums for Magical Threats

Blaze of Secrets (AMT #1)

Frozen Desires (AMT #2)

Shadow of Temptation (AMT #3)

Flare of Promise (AMT #4)

Cascade Shifters

Convincing the Cougar (CS #0.5)

Reclaiming the Wolf (CS #1)

Cougar's First Christmas (CS #2)

Resisting the Cougar (CS #3)

Love in Scotland

Crazy Scottish Love (LiS #1)

Chaotic Scottish Wedding (LiS #2)

WRITING AS LIZZIE ENGLAND

(Super sexy contemporary novellas)

Her Fantasy

Holt: The CEO

Callan: The Highlander

Adam: The Duke

Gabe: The Rock Star

About the Author

Jessie Donovan has sold over half a million books, has given away hundreds of thousands more to readers for free, and has even hit the *NY Times* and *USA Today* bestseller lists. She is best known for her dragon-shifter series, but also writes about magic users, aliens, and even has a crazy romantic comedy series set in Scotland. When not reading a book, attempting to tame her yard, or traipsing around some foreign country on a shoestring, she can often be found interacting with her readers on Facebook. She lives near Seattle, where, yes, it rains a lot but it also makes everything green.

Printed in Great Britain
by Amazon

26268731R00078